Ehvah After

Rose Dee

Hole in the Wind Publishing

Ehvah After

Formatting by: Wild Seas Formatting
(http://www.WildSeasFormatting.com)

Hole in the Wind Publishing

Dedication:

For my son, Tully.

Acknowledgements

My name may be on the front cover, but many people helped me along the way.

Thank you to:

My wonderful husband, Terry, and the best son a mother could ever have, Tully. My simply stupendous editor, Iola Goulton – I'd be lost without you; my talented friends and co-authors, Paula Vince and Amanda Deed, and best proofer in the world, Michelle Evans. Thank you to all my readers: My mum - Mary Venables; my sister - Leonie Turner; Georgina Elford, and Mary Preece. A grateful thanks to Rik Hall for his expert formatting skills, advice, and help. Thank you to Rosanna White for sharing her amazing talent and producing an outstanding cover.

Above all, my humble and grateful thanks to my Heavenly Father for giving me all I need to work this writing ministry.

CHAPTER 1

"I can't believe how horrible it was tonight. I don't know why I bother going to these things." Ehvah Rowe flipped the car visor down and groaned at the sight of her knotted hair in the tiny mirror.

"I know. The paparazzi were nasty." Ritchie pulled the sports car around a series of Beverly Hills corners. Palm trees flashed in the headlights as he braked.

Ehvah fingered the hair extensions in an effort to improve her appearance, then flipped the visor back up.

"You could have grabbed me before I fell. Now the whole world will think I'm back on the clubbing scene."

"Aren't you? This is the third club we've been to this week."

Ehvah let a long sigh escape. "Only because you insisted we go. The tabloids must be sick of printing photos of me leaving clubs. Besides, I hadn't stepped foot in one for over a month before you dragged me back in. I'm sick of my bad press."

"You can't blame me for your fallen princess rep. You got that title all on your own, dahling." Ritchie changed gears as they climbed a hill.

"Don't remind me. Sometimes I wish I could re-do the last two years."

Ehvah closed her eyes in the hope that the pitch black would block out her mistakes.

"I can't go back to clubbing every night, Ritchie. No matter how much you love the scene. There's nothing in it for me any more."

"So what are you going to do? Your singing career didn't take off. Are you going to try to get back into acting?"

Ehvah contemplated his question. Her successful years on a TV sitcom may have scored her a teen queen title and a few hit singles, but the fame was long gone. The time she had spent out of the entertainment industry had produced nothing but a fallen star persona.

"I want to sing, but I just can't break though. The last time I met with a recording company, they told me I had a great voice, heaps of talent, and a fine heritage, but I didn't fit into any of their current successful molds. Nothing much has changed in the last two years, so what's the use?"

She had been devastated to be pegged as a has-been at the age of twenty-two. At the time she had settled for being a professional party girl. Now it was obvious that career move had been useless.

"I have no idea what to do, but anything is better than being tabloid fodder."

Ritchie pulled into the long driveway of the two-story Beverly Hills house she shared with Aunt Mara and her fourth husband, James.

"Turn off the lights and try to sneak around the back entrance," Ehvah said as they approached the building. "I don't want James to know I'm home."

The last thing she needed was an encounter with her uncle. Besides, the two cars parked in the front driveway meant he was busy with clients.

"Does he hate you for coming in late all the time?"

Ritchie slowed and pulled around the back.

"James is usually cool, but last week when I got in late, we kind of had an argument. I'd like to avoid another one." She didn't want to retell the embarrassing story.

Ritchie was undeterred by her vague answer. He gave her a "come on, spill it" glance.

Ehvah picked at one long acrylic fingernail and resigned herself to the inevitable.

"The heel broke on one of those crazy high stilettos you insisted I wear. I grabbed hold of that huge vase in the foyer, but it was too late. I ended up on the floor, and the vase shattered into a million pieces. James came running out of his den and had to scrape me off the floor. He told me I needed to get a new hobby."

"Not the shoes from the Vogue shoot? They were superb." Ritchie stopped the car and cringed.

"Yes, those shoes. I know he meant well, but the whole thing set me off. As if I don't know my life is in turmoil. The last thing I need is him pointing out the obvious."

"And you were wearing that cut-out dress. Do you think he saw anything?" He slapped his hands to his cheeks.

Ehvah contemplated her outfit that night. It was skin-tight, and short. James's other unwelcome comment that she "needed to rethink her wardrobe" revealed he was unimpressed with Ritchie's fashion pick to match the shoes.

"No. It was tight enough to keep my vanity in check, but he must have seen my tattoo because he made a comment about young celebrities thinking it's cool to mark their bodies." She rolled her eyes. "It made me so angry. I hate it when he acts all fatherly towards me. I know he means well, but sometimes he forgets that it's my house and I pay the bills. I can do what I like."

She swallowed hard in an effort to quell the memory of why she held sole responsibility for her life.

"Tattoo? I didn't know you had a tattoo." Ritchie raised one eyebrow.

"It's private. James only knows about it because he looks after my money and he picked up the transaction on my credit card, years ago." Ehvah reached down to grab her purse. She didn't want to discuss her one tiny inking with Ritchie.

"I don't know why you put up with them."

"Because he's usually sweet and supportive. He's the main reason I still let Mara stay in my house. That, and she always throws it back in my face that she's the only family I have left." She reached for the door handle. "Anyway, James is way too good for her. She treats him horribly."

"True."

"Now if it was Lyle who had been helping me, that would be a different story. I can't stand that greasy pig." Her aunt's personal assistant was a dirty, slimy snake. Ehvah felt his eyes undressing her the second she was in his company.

"He is a bit too suave." Ritchie screwed up one corner of his mouth in clear support of her assessment.

"Shopping tomorrow?" Ehvah asked as she stuffed her cell phone into her purse.

"Can't. I'm on an early shoot. Apparently they need someone to fetch belts, hang clothes and make coffee." He waved his hands up in dramatic fashion. "If I'm really lucky, I'll get to spray tan the model. Yay."

His sarcasm made Ehvah smile.

"We should try that new club over on Vine. I hear it's becoming quite the celebrity hangout." Ritchie flicked on the interior light.

Ehvah swallowed hard. She had no desire to step foot in another club for the rest of her life, but how could she tell Ritchie that? He lived to be seen.

During her working years, the entire entertainment industry had touted her as one of the most consummate young professionals in the business. She had never indulged in the usual teenage antics. The club scene, drugs, and popular crowds had never appealed to her. She had dated a little and had a few boyfriends, but nothing long-term. Now she had indulged in some catch-up teenage rebellion, she yearned to return to a productive existence. But what did that entail?

She shrugged. "I'll call you tomorrow."

"Goodnight, princess," Richie called as he pulled away from the house.

Ehvah continued towards the house without turning to acknowledge him. Ritchie was a recent addition to her life. Unlike her, he had grown up in the L.A. party scene and had latched on to her six months ago when she had been venturing out at night. She had him pegged as an attention seeker. Being seen with a celebrity, even a secondhand one like her, was what Ritchie was all about. The fact she paid for everything helped. Ritchie wasn't a real friend, but still, it was nice to have someone. Even if it was someone who was using her.

Ehvah threw her purse on the nearest bench and closed the door.

The extensive kitchen glowed eerie shadows in the night light. With the help gone for the day, the bustling area was dead, apart from the hum of many white goods. Reflections from stainless steel benches lit her way to the foyer.

Ehvah moved through the foyer, pulling off her heels in an effort to negotiate the marble floor without sound.

She was halfway across the room when voices echoed through a slit in the den door. She couldn't hear what was being said, but the tones were male.

As she reached the staircase a sparkle caught her eye.

My earring.

She had made an extensive search for the lost diamond drop, to no avail. It must have dislodged during her fall last week. She bent down to peer into a crack on the bottom step of the oak staircase. A few tiny chips of porcelain from the broken vase were scattered around the lost diamond. Lucky for her, the hired help hadn't done their jobs properly this week. She went behind the staircase and dropped onto all fours to retrieve the jewel. As she did, the voices in the den got louder.

"Here! This is all you need. Take everything."

It was James. The high pitch in his voice was unnatural for the docile man.

"We will," another male voice said.

Several loud pops followed.

Ehvah froze as the door widened. Through the slits in the staircase, she saw three men exit.

She could feel her breath sitting heavy on her chest as the last man paused at the doorway to tuck a hand gun into his belt. The thin stream of light from the den beamed onto his torso, and darkness covered his face. As he turned to walk away, the illumination revealed a tattoo protruding from the back of his shirt collar. A black snake's head twisted out of the rim of his t-shirt and up to his hairline.

Ehvah held her breath, hoping the shadows would hide her.

The man paused for a moment, then exited via the main door.

Ehvah stayed where she was, not willing or able to move. She swallowed hard, feeling pins and needles run up her body from the tip of her toes to each follicle on her scalp.

Sounds of car doors closing and engines starting were followed by the gritty rolling of tires on the driveway.

When the engines faded, Ehvah inched out from under the staircase. She paused, aware of the pain in her knees from resting on the hard surface. The indent of one porcelain chip marked her shin.

The silence was deafening. An overwhelming feeling that she had to do something flooded her conscience, but a fog of confusion and indecision rooted her to the spot.

She willed herself forward, tiptoeing towards the den.

"James? James? Are you alright?"

Even as she said the words, a sick bubble in her stomach erupted and lodged in her throat.

She could feel her body start to shake, as undeniable horror drove her forward and she pushed the door wide.

The scream that sounded within deafened her far more than the disjointed gurgle that came out of her mouth.

James sat back in his leather seat, his lips parted, and eyes wide. Two holes cratered on his forehead, and a trickle of blood ran red down his face.

CHAPTER 2

Ehvah could see her hands shaking, but was unable to control them. It was as though her entire body kept fixing in a state of shock. Another chill ran down her spine as she felt her shoulders shudder.

"You need to pull yourself together. This has affected me too. I'm suffering. I've lost a husband." Aunt Mara twisted a handkerchief and stifled another sob.

Ehvah sensed her aunt's drama queen act was purely display. A show of being distraught was something she frequently pulled to get her own way.

"It's not the first time you've lost a partner. Maybe you should spend more time with them, then they wouldn't leave. Let's at least hope James is in a better place." Ehvah couldn't stop the sarcastic comment from bursting out. Since her aunt had arrived and begun her grieving widow act, Ehvah had wished the woman was already on the plane heading back to Australia, where she was currently working.

Mara's ice-blue eyes fixed on her. All sobbing ceased and her dark lashes flicked a clear message of displeasure.

"How could you be so cruel? I'm the only family you have left. James understood why I wasn't with him. This is my chance for a comeback. It's the role of a lifetime. He encouraged me to go to Australia."

Ehvah slumped over the padded armrest of the hotel chair. At least Mara had caught the first plane back home.

Her aunt reached over to pick up a glass of water. There was an edgy flicker in her fingers. Maybe she really was rattled.

Ehvah looked out the hotel window at the L.A. city view.

It was over forty-eight hours since she had found James. She was a mess when the police had arrived. They had taken her to hospital for treatment.

"How long have you been here?"

Mara's question pulled her back to reality.

"I'm not sure." Everything since finding James was a blur. "The doctor wanted me to stay in hospital longer, but the place was doing my head in. He put me on medication and let me check in here. He's coming to see me this afternoon."

She looked up at her aunt. "I can't go back to the house." Ehvah wondered for a moment if she would ever set foot in her own mansion again.

Mara closed her eyes and stretched her neck. Her long black hair swept to each shoulder as she tilted her head.

"Well, I can't possibly afford the time to do anything for you. I have a funeral to plan, and if I don't get back on set as soon as possible, that rotten director will replace me." She put the glass back on the table with more force than necessary.

"I've already sent Lyle over to the house to collect some important documents for me. I can arrange for the help to bring you over anything you need."

Mara's offer was pitiful, but Ehvah wasn't going to turn down a chance for her aunt to do something positive for her, even if that was just issuing orders to others.

"You can ask him to pack me some clothes, and bring the photo of me and my parents on my bedside table. Everything else can stay there for now."

Besides the necessities, she had no idea what she might want.

Mara re-crossed her long legs. Ehvah thought how different she was to her half-sister, Ehvah's mother, in both looks and nature. Ehvah shared her mother's blonde hair, medium height, slim figure and modest chest. Mara was a carbon copy of her own actress mother, Ehvah's grandfather's second wife: tall, dark, with angular cheekbones, and large chest.

"Are you ready to talk about what you saw? I'd like to

know if you can do something to bring my husband's murderer to justice." Mara set her mouth into one thin line.

Ehvah squirmed under her glare. The appeal sounded reasonable, but her aunt's lack of emotion was unnerving. But cold and calculating was Mara's general approach to all things in life.

"I didn't see much." She shifted her weight in the chair, which should have been comfortable, but became as hard as a rock under Mara's scrutiny.

"I had just gotten home and was under the stairs, picking up the earring I lost last week, when I heard the shots. Three men came out. One tucked a gun under his belt and they left. I have no idea who they were. It was too dark to see their faces."

Saying it out loud did strange things to her insides. A horrible sick feeling swirled around her stomach.

Mara squinted.

"What about James? Did you hear him say anything specific to these men?"

Ehvah closed her eyes and tried to recall the moments before the shots, before seeing James lifeless. She shook her head. "He said they could have it all. Something like that."

"Nothing else?"

"I don't think so."

"Are you sure you didn't see who they were? Not one face or defining feature?"

The image of a black snake flashed before her eyes. It was interrupted by the ringing of the hotel phone on the table next to her aunt.

Mara answered. "Yes?"

There was a pause.

"Is this necessary? My niece is suffering from shock and needs time to recover."

Who was calling?

"What involvement do you have with my husband's murder?" Mara stood up and paced as she spoke.

There was another pause before Mara's chest heaved.

"Fine. I'll let her know you're coming, but you can wait

until her doctor visits her this afternoon."

She slammed the phone back on its cradle.

"Apparently, you're to have a visit from the FBI."

***

Back in her hotel room, Mara could feel a stress migraine threaten to explode behind her forehead.

Her entire world was threatening to crumble in front of her eyes.

"Two years, Lyle. Two years I've been planning this." She grabbed a scarf hanging over a chair and wrung the fabric tight. "Are you telling me it's all gone?"

"I don't know how it happened, but I know it's not there." Lyle sat on the edge of his chair and quickened the pace of his bouncing leg. His show of nervous energy stoked the rage in her gut.

"Well, where is it?"

"I don't know." Lyle stared at the hotel room ceiling. "Whoever killed James must have something to do with it. With the FBI crawling all over us, it's going to be hard to find out where it is."

Mara rubbed a hand over her face in an effort to clear her head. She was so close to the life she wanted, yet now it felt as though every risk she had taken was for nothing. The burning inside morphed into a swirl of panic as the memory of her mother produced a vibrant shaking inside. There was one thing she wouldn't let happen.

"Lyle, you had better find my money, because I am not going to be like my mother, an out-of-work actress at the mercy of a string of pathetic men. I can't believe James would transfer that money unless he had to. We have to find out where he's put it."

She threw the scarf back over the chair.

"I've put up with Ehvah and her reluctant charity for long enough. We need to buy some time. I'm certain we've missed something."

Mara considered her husband's character. James had always been obedient. Perhaps the answer lay elsewhere.

"Maybe there's something she's not telling us."

Lyle ran a hand through his slicked-back hair.

"Do you think she knows more than she's letting on?"

"I don't know."

Mara studied the same view as her niece, except Ehvah was several floors above her in a better room. The thought of her second-rate position flared a spark of determination.

"We need to keep her confined until we can figure it out."

Lyle rose to straighten his suit. His lean form and medium height complimented the attire.

"We'll work it out, babe."

Mara took in the details of his much younger face. Despite his dandy style, he looked like a boy. She huffed.

"I'll work it out. You need to do as you're told. As for Ehvah, she has to play our game. Right now, the less she talks, the better."

CHAPTER 3

Ehvah licked her dry lips and pushed down the rising anxiety. Holding her emotions in check was hard enough, now she had to deal with hard-faced FBI Agent Gregson.

Gregson was a small woman. Her black bobbed hair, sharp-cut suit and direct manner were unnerving. She sat on the couch, flipped her notepad over and glanced at her male colleague. He left the room before she spoke.

"So you came to live with your aunt after the sudden death of both your parents, and then soon after them, your paternal grandmother?"

Ehvah felt the tightness in her chest constrict.

"That's right. My parents died in a small plane crash, and not long after that my grandmother suffered a fatal heart attack." She stopped to take a deep breath, hoping the extra oxygen would quell the rising indignation towards this woman. It didn't work. "Have you people lived under a rock for the last ten years? You do know who my parents were, right? Please tell me the FBI isn't completely clueless."

Gregson's grey eyes met hers.

"Yes, we do know your background, Miss Rowe, but a general overview is an important first step in an interview such as this. Please humor us."

Ehvah felt hot liquid collect under her bottom lashes. She rubbed her eyes in an attempt to force the tears of frustration away.

Gregson addressed her notepad. Ehvah wondered why she bothered writing at all when a recording device sat on the table between them. It was just another aspect of this interview that irritated her.

"It will be easier if I do the background run through. I'll need verbal confirmation from you when I indicate. Okay?" Gregson paused and looked up.

Ehvah took a deep controlled breath and nodded. "Yes."

"Your parents were popular singing and songwriting team, Evan and Reevah Rowe. After their sudden deaths, you lived with your father's mother, who had helped raise you from birth. She suffered a heart attack a short time later and by default you came to live with Mara, your half-aunt and your only living relative." She looked up for confirmation.

"That's correct."

Gregson continued. "Your parent's earnings are controlled by a trust fund. You receive a monthly allowance from this source. The fund is to be fully released to you on your twenty-fifth birthday, which is one year from now. The trust also controls all ongoing royalties attributed to your parents' music portfolio."

Her parents' number one hit, *Forever Yours*, still held the record for the highest-selling duet. Ehvah wouldn't listen to it, but did occasionally hear it by accident. It brought back too many devastating memories, like her name which was an amalgamation of her parent's names. In true celebrity style, they recreated the word Ever to Ehvah.

She took another breath. "Yes."

"Apart from this trust fund, which is independently controlled, you also have significant earnings from your past acting and singing career, including ongoing royalties. James controlled this portfolio on your behalf."

"Yes."

"Were you aware of James's other business dealings, considering he lived primarily in your house with your aunt, and had an office there?"

Ehvah shook her head. "I rarely discussed money with James. He kept me informed and I trusted him. I didn't know he had other business interests, let alone anything illegal."

"How long have James and your aunt lived with you?"

Ehvah blinked hard, trying to recall the answer.

"Mara moved into a guardianship role when my grandmother died ten years ago, but apart from the initial push into my acting career, she never took any interest in me. My manager steered my career."

"And he passed away three years ago, right?"

Looked like Gregson has done her homework after all.

"That's right. Mara had two unsuccessful marriages through my working years. I rarely had anything to do with her. She basically lived off me because she couldn't land an acting job. So long as she stayed out of my way, I didn't care."

She hadn't been living with her aunt long before realizing Mara's personal ambitions were Mara's first and only priority.

"She met and married James just before my manager died. I liked James. He was a nice guy."

Ehvah recalled the warm conversations she had had with her uncle. It had been obvious that Mara had no idea how smart and caring he was. Unfortunately for James, he had been starstruck by her aunt's beauty, and had confused her real character with the loving heroine Mara had played in one of her early b-grade movies.

"James took over my financial management when my sitcom ended."

Gregson jotted in her notebook.

"Is your aunt employed by you in any capacity?"

"No way. The only reason I've let Mara stay with me is because of James, and she knows it. It's obvious she's been having an affair with Lyle, her toy-boy assistant, but she wouldn't divorce James. She knows that if she did, she'd be on her own."

Gregson tilted her head, dislodging the neat angle of her bob.

"So, financially, you look after both your aunt and uncle?"

"I paid James a salary, and let them live in one wing of the house. I rarely see Mara. She's been filming in Australia for the last month."

Ehvah rolled her eyes at her aunt's self-professed career comeback. Industry insiders had told her that the underfunded financiers had been forced to settle with her aunt for a pivotal role, but that the talented up-and-coming director was furious with the decision.

"Did James ever discuss his marriage with you?"

Ehvah tried to tap into recollections of past heart-to-hearts with her uncle.

"Not really. But it was obvious he knew about Mara and Lyle. He . . ."

Loud voices and a slamming door in the suite's foyer cut her off.

"I want to speak to my niece."

Mara barraged into the room, followed by Agent Gregson's colleague, who looked frazzled.

"I tried to stop her." He appealed to his superior.

Gregson placed her notebook and pen by her side. "I'll be a few more minutes."

Mara stood her ground. "I insist I speak to her now. Alone."

Gregson expelled a deep breath and left the room. Mara took her vacated seat.

"Ehvah, I'm going to give you some advice and you need to take it."

Ehvah screwed up one side of her mouth.

Mara started at her, cold blue eyes flickering with the reflections of lamp light.

"Tell the FBI as little as possible. If you don't, they'll take your life. You're vulnerable right now. You need to protect yourself."

Mara rarely offered helpful advice. This was one time she was opening with a targeted argument.

Ehvah took one look at her shaking hands. It was confirmation that she needed to at least consider what Mara was saying.

"You don't even have legal representation. If you're not careful, these people will have you in a witness protection program for years. How are you going to get your career back if they force you into hiding?"

Ehvah's heart thumped at the thought of years on the run.

"If you don't shut up, the killers will get to you. You've

seen the movies."

Mara was right. Ehvah needed to be careful with her eyewitness recount. The thought of another encounter with the killers made her skin crawl. She could feel the sweat running down the small of her back and the thumping in her ears morphing into one long thud.

Ehvah nodded. She decided to take Mara's advice and tell Agent Gregson she had heard the shots, but had seen nothing. It wasn't a complete lie—she hadn't seen any of their faces. The exterior security cameras would give them a physical description of the three men. They didn't need her.

CHAPTER 4

Mara tried to get comfortable on the old leather bench. A sharp pain pounded her forehead. The situation was bad enough, but the added heat of tropical northern Australia, combined with the weight of the massive Victorian period costume she was wearing, made the throbbing between her temples unbearable.

"This place is the pits."

Lyle cringed.

"When you said tropical northern Australia, I thought you meant beaches, islands and paradise, not the middle of the rainforest."

Mara fingered her heavy costume. The folds of her petticoat took up most of the space on the curved sofa. This was supposed to be her big comeback. A period drama set in fashionable Australia. In reality, she was stuck in the rainforest in the mountains above Cairns on location shoots.

"There's some catching up due to James's death. When they don't need me I can retreat to the beach house they rented in Cairns."

Lyle gave up trying to cool himself, so unbuttoned his shirt, then peeled it away from his sweaty form. Mara felt a stirring of desire at the sight of his bare chest.

"Where's Ehvah?" He fanned his armpits.

"In a hotel. It was the best I could do on short notice. At least she's here. If I hadn't barged in on that interview, we'd be stuck in the States babysitting her. No doubt the FBI would have forced us all to stay in the country. At the moment, the further away from the situation I get, the better it is for me." She pulled at a petticoat seam that sweat had stuck to her thigh.

Lyle screwed up one side of his mouth as Mara continued.

"It's going to be annoying having her around, but I don't see that I had much choice. If I didn't get back here, they would've recast me for sure. We need to buy some time. Maybe with us all out of the country, the FBI will go off the scent."

"Until we find the money, we'll need Ehvah's to keep us going. Maybe it was a bad idea to put every cent into that shelf company. There had to be a better option for a legitimate business facade." He loosened his belt.

His critical statement sent a hot flash coursing through her body.

"If we don't find out where that money is, we'll lose everything."

"I don't know what else to do." Lyle paced the floor of the old location trailer. His deep strides covered its length in seconds.

"Find it."

She could feel a torrent of abuse sitting on the surface of her tongue.

Lyle paused from his pacing and ran a hand through his highlighted hair. It looked uncharacteristically disheveled. Clumps of product had separated the neat slicked-back look Lyle favored, and three-day growth prickled his usually clean shaven profile.

Mara gave him a cursory glance. His overall appearance was unbecoming.

"I suggest you do something about the way you look. Go and shave at least. You're revealing your heritage." Lyle's background was shady. His family was in the business of illegal gambling, and Lyle was considered underwhelming by his successful criminal clan.

"I'd rather not discuss my family. They scare me."

Mara set her gaze on him. "At least your delinquent cousins would know where to start looking for my missing bank account."

Lyle took a seat on the narrow bench beside her and

slumped forward over the table. "I told you, I've looked everywhere for the information. Every drawer, every computer, every file. I even went through his entire wardrobe."

"Why on earth did James transfer the money in the first place?" Mara could feel her frustration mounting to breaking point.

"He must have known they were onto us." Lyle paused to sigh. "Well, onto him anyway."

Mara reached behind to flick the clunker of an air conditioner up higher. "I just hope they don't figure out our involvement." A flutter of fear crept in before she pushed it back down. "But then, I suppose if they knew about us, we'd already be dead."

Lyle shuffled a little closer. "You played it so well, I'm certain no one suspected a thing. You should win an Oscar for that grieving widow performance." He raised one corner of his mouth in a sneak's salute.

Mara reached out and patted his prickly cheek. "I was pretty good, wasn't I?"

"You were brilliant, babe. From the tears at the funeral to the FBI interrogation, you didn't falter once."

"Well, it was a shock to find out that they had been watching James. Thank goodness they didn't get close enough to discover us." She lifted one side of an old curtain. "At least being stuck in this hole of a place has its advantages."

"How much longer do you have on this shoot?" Lyle flapped his arms again.

"Another month on location here, then one more location west of here. Apparently it gets hotter the further you travel inland. That's something to look forward to."

A rustle outside sounded over the hum of the air conditioner, and she placed a finger on her lips to silence him. A knock on the door of the trailer followed, along with the call for her presence on set.

Mara pulled her mammoth dress out of the seat.

"Don't second-guess James's business talent. This didn't fall apart because of him. You got sloppy, and he paid the price. I just hope the crime mob don't piece together your movements and link you to the scheme. James will have the money safely deposited. We just have to find out where." She pointed the finger at him. "You have to find out where."

Lyle cringed at the command. "Do you want me to go down to Cairns? I could question Ehvah. She might have remembered something else, something that could help us?"

"What! Send you to Cairns so you can hit on her? I'm not stupid. You place one foot wrong with her, and you can kiss our arrangement goodbye. I pulled you out of oblivion. I can throw you back there."

She opened the door and pulled the folds of the dress through the tiny opening, before leaning back in.

"Sit tight until I can come up with something," she whispered.

CHAPTER 5

Ehvah looked out the hotel window at the Pacific Ocean view. Yesterday had been warm and sunny. She had taken a cab down to the nearest beach and spent an afternoon being enveloped by the welcoming Australian sun.

It was the perfect day of relaxation until she stumbled on the road and narrowly missed being hit by a car.

Today was a dramatic change. Heavy winds whipped up an ocean full of white caps, and dark rain clouds threatened from a distance.

She pulled her attention away from the lounge window and back to the man sitting across from her. The local real estate agent had helped her when she had fallen the day before, and today had shown her every property he had for holiday rental, but nothing had felt right.

"Are you sure there's nothing else?"

The real estate agent flicked through his list.

"Nothing I haven't already shown you."

Phil Smith was a tall, older man with a fit physique and bald head. After having run into him yesterday, Phil had sold her on the idea of spending her holiday time in a house instead of a hotel. The move made sense to her. Security was tighter in a controlled environment.

"None of the properties you've shown me are suitable. I guess I'm stuck here for now."

Her hotel room wasn't ideal, but at least it was a beautiful place to be. The property sat on the oceanfront in Cairns, and her view incorporated green spits full of mangrove trees bordering a water inlet.

In the two weeks she had been here, she had spent a

lot of time sitting in her room watching the boating activity. Fishing vessels and pleasure boats frequented the waterway. Even a government customs boat had gone by. It was silver and sleek, nothing like the weathered commercial vessels with their balls of shrimp net on each side, or stacked dinghies on their decks.

Phil closed his file and picked his cell phone up off the table.

"Don't give up on me yet. I still have a few places that might work out. I have your contact details, so I'll be in touch soon. Don't worry."

Ehvah walked him to the door. "I appreciate you dropping everything to help me."

"Not a problem." Phil enclosed her hand in a firm shake. "It was a pleasure, Ms. Rowe. What are your movements in the next few days? Can I contact you here tomorrow?"

"Yes, I'll be here for now, but I'm not sure what I'm doing long-term. I may have to go back home at any moment." Agent Gregson's warning that she may be needed back in the States was forefront in her thoughts.

Phil paused with his hand on the door handle. "I've heard about your recent trouble. It must have been shocking."

Ehvah held her breath. Phil hadn't brought up James or the situation she had run away from. She shuffled her feet, trying to buy some time to piece together a reply.

"It was hard. My aunt convinced me to come here. She says Australia will do me good." She tried to form a smile, but was certain it came out forced.

Phil must have picked up on her reluctance to discuss her personal situation because he moved to open the door.

"Well, I'm sure we can find you that private property with the heightened security system you want. I just need some time to explore a few options."

"Sounds great." Ehvah held the door as he moved into the hallway. "The last thing I need is the paparazzi finding me here. It's only a matter of time before one of the staff alerts them."

"Don't worry, your location is safe with me. I won't give

you up." Phil tucked his leather satchel under his arm.

"I appreciate that." Ehvah allowed a deep breath to escape.

She said goodbye, closed the door, and made her way into the separate bedroom. It was a small miracle she hadn't already been found out.

There was no doubt that the public scrutiny would have been far worse if she had stayed in America. Taking Mara's advice and following her back to Australia was one way of avoiding a lot of things, including James's murderers.

Ehvah had kept the snake tattoo to herself, not even telling Mara about it. Anyway, the cameras would have picked up that identifying feature. Wouldn't they? Concealing the information had seemed like a good way to make it go away. It hadn't. It had grown bigger and scarier as each day passed.

Ehvah shook her head in the hope of removing all events from her mind. She reached over to the bedside table to retrieve her cell phone and check her social media sites. The screen revealed nothing but photos of Ritchie with his new best friend, a hip, young model. Ehvah deleted the status updates, then un-friended Ritchie.

Good riddance.

Ritchie had been happy to hang around when she was an out-of-control party girl, but he had run for the hills the second Ehvah became a disturbed and fearful murder witness, telling her he couldn't deal with her damage.

She wasn't fooled. Ritchie couldn't deal with her not funding his party lifestyle any more.

She threw her phone down and grabbed the journal she had purchased that morning, writing the words, *Ehvah After* on the inside cover. It was the ritual she had adopted for each new journal. *Ehvah After* was the last song her parents had written before their plane had crashed. It was a sweet love song to her. It was never recorded.

Every year on the anniversary of their deaths, she had to endure the commentary of fans and industry insiders talking about her parent's great love story, like there was some sort of satisfaction that they were together in death as they were in life. Ehvah hated it. Just because her parents had believed in God didn't mean their deaths should be celebrated. She certainly didn't celebrate being without them.

She paused to recall what her grandmother had told her the day of their funeral—that trusting in God wasn't always easy, because bad things happen, and we may never understand why. But if we did decide to trust, He would be faithful and give us all we needed.

She still didn't understand what that meant, and when Gran died of a heart attack, she didn't know who to trust. It wasn't that she didn't believe God existed; she just wasn't sure she could trust Him.

Don't you realize I'm all alone? Where are you?

She closed her journal and placed it on the bed beside her. Journaling was a habit she had started when Gran died. It had been a vital part of her life. One thing she did trust were the recordings of her emotions. It was therapy. There had even been attempts to put some of her writing to music, but with little success. That particular talent had passed her by.

She picked at some nuts on the bedside table, as huge raindrops pelted the window. It had been a struggle to eat anything substantial since finding James.

In spite of the medication the doctor back home had given her, sleep was as elusive as her appetite. Her dreams were filled with death or snakes. She could feel her shock giving way to fear.

The melodic tune of her cell phone broke through the now-thundering torrent outside. It was her aunt.

She had been so close to breaking all ties with Mara. Now drastic circumstances had thrown them together again.

"Yes?"

Ehvah didn't even try to be pleasant.

"I've organized a change of venue for your vacation."

"Excuse me?"

"I'm moving you to the beach house the production company has rented. I've cleared it with them. They're not using it. It's just up the coast. You'll love it. It's the perfect secluded place. I've organized security to go with it."

Ehvah couldn't believe the audacity of the woman.

"I can organize my own life, thank you." She wished her aunt would leave her alone to think.

"Don't be a brat. It's all organized. You'll be much more comfortable."

Ehvah stood up and paced the length of the room.

"I can take care of my own accommodation." She didn't want to be beholden to her aunt for anything.

"If you could take care of yourself, you wouldn't have ended up in hospital yesterday. I thought you were keeping a low profile."

Ehvah let out an exasperated breath, as though the energy release would somehow help alleviate her frustration.

"I did not end up in hospital. I had a tiny graze. I was taken to the medical center. The doctor cleaned up my scrapes and gave me the all clear. I used a false name. Anyway, how do you know about that?"

"Your guest services man mentioned it. What about the paparazzi? How many photos did they get?"

Ehvah threw a pillow at the wall.

"None. Anyway, he wasn't a paparazzo. He was a real estate agent taking scenic shots of the area, and a nice guy. He took me to the medical center, and he's been showing me properties to rent today."

Ehvah stood to pace in front of the window. Her accident at the beach yesterday had upset her, but she had no intention of sharing the details with Mara. "Since when did you take an interest in my life? First you're worried about my safety back home, now you're concerned about paparazzi here? Why are you questioning the hotel staff about me? What gives?"

Ehvah heard a loud huff.

"I told you it was best to stay in the hotel. I don't know why you'd go to the beach when you have a nice private pool to sunbathe by."

Ehvah couldn't believe what she was hearing. First Mara has the hotel staff spying on her, now she thinks she's entitled to give advice.

"Who are you? My keeper? If I want to go to the beach, I will. Besides, I wasn't sunbathing. I went for a walk. This is Australia, for goodness sake. Why wouldn't I go to the beach? The accident was not my fault. I forgot these people drive on the wrong side of the road." She reached down and touched a sore spot where she had fallen.

"I'm trying to be nice, Ehvah. I suggested you come here because I feel partly responsible for what you've suffered. If I had been aware of what James was doing this wouldn't have happened. Won't you at least let me try and make it up to you? We are family, after all."

Mara didn't play nice. There was always an ulterior motive. A flood of regret ran through her. Escaping the scrutiny of the FBI and running away from James's killers back home had dumped her with her scheming, manipulative aunt. Which was worse?

She didn't have the energy to dissect her aunt's motives. Not only was she plagued with nightmares of the snake tattoo, her anxiety had increased to a level she hadn't experienced since her parents had died. Her life was slipping away into a mass of deathly thoughts, and she was all alone.

There was a long pause before Mara spoke in soft, deliberate tones.

"Maybe it's taken this horrible event for me to realize how valuable you are to me."

"What do you mean?"

"Well . . . with James's death, and your little brush with disaster yesterday, I'm realizing how alone I am in the world. You're the only family I have left."

The words were nice, but the tone was off. Mara wasn't that good an actress, despite her self-opinionated view of her talent.

On the other hand, whatever Mara's hidden motivations, at least someone was interested in her wellbeing, even if it was Mara. Ehvah weighed up her options: stay at the hotel and be spied on, go back to the States and face the FBI, as well as increasing media interest in the murder, or go to the isolated beach house—an idea she had been pursuing with Phil anyway.

The last option was by far the best. It would give her time to consider her next move—her aunt's motives—and having some security around her was a good idea. Maybe a sense of safety would help dispel her fear.

"Okay, I'll go. It will give me the privacy I need to deal with all of this. I should have told the FBI about those men. It's driving me crazy."

"We've been over this. If you keep your mouth shut and disappear for a bit everything will settle down and we can both get on with our lives."

"Just what was James into? You must have suspected something."

There was a pause on the line.

"I don't know the full story, which is probably why I'm still alive. The FBI wouldn't tell me anything. I need to get on with my job. You've had your turn in the spotlight. This is my chance."

Ehvah smiled. That was the real Mara.

"Alright, I'll use the beach house, and the security".

"Good girl. Just leave all your things and I'll send someone over to pack them up for you. I don't want you to worry about a thing."

Ehvah rolled her eyes. Compliance always brought out the best in her aunt.

CHAPTER 6

Mara couldn't mask the smile on her face as she disconnected her call from Ehvah. Her obstinate niece was playing her game for once. She glanced up at Lyle while retrieving a number from her cell phone.

"Fear can be a wonderful ally."

Lyle paused in his task of making coffee in her trailer's kitchenette.

"She's going to the house?"

Mara nodded as the call she placed was answered.

"Northern Security? I spoke to you earlier. I want to go ahead with the job we discussed. There's one aspect I would like to reiterate."

"Yes, certainly."

The man's voice held an agreeable tone.

"My niece is extremely troubled. She's suffering from shock and is on strong medication. Your staff must monitor her every movement. Do you understand?"

"That's not a problem. The man I've organized is very good at his job. He'll be there on a permanent basis, except for some overnight relief. Your niece will be well taken care of."

Mara fingered the envelope of the letter she had received just a few hours ago.

"She had better be. I want a report twice a day. Any outings she plans to take must be approved by me first. She's in a fragile emotional state, and not capable of making any decisions."

"I understand."

Mara disconnected the call before grabbing her vanity

case and turning to Lyle.

"Here's the plan."

***

Ehvah picked up the hotel phone.

"Ms. Rowe, we have a man from Northern Security here to collect you. Can we send him up?"

Ehvah checked the clock in her hotel room foyer. It was one hour since her conversation with Mara about moving to the house. The transfer had arrived too soon. When Mara pushed for something, she went hard.

"Tell him to come up in ten minutes."

Ehvah glanced around the room, wondering where to start. First, Phil Smith. It was common courtesy to inform him his services were no longer required. The agent assured her he knew of the property. It was set in the prime location for celebrities, and was perfect for her needs.

With this reassurance, Ehvah started organizing her belongings.

The doorbell rang and she spied through the peephole to make sure the caller was the security man she was expecting.

The man's bulk filled the distorted vision of the spyglass. Ehvah followed the line of his body from the oversized loafers on his feet, to his casual jeans. A suit jacket covered broad shoulders, and a thick neck flowed on from the curve of his t-shirt collar. Strong square jawline, slightly crooked nose and—

Ehvah jerked away from the door. He was staring straight at her, right down the peephole.

She felt a little shiver run down her spine. There was no mistaking this man for anything but security. She smoothed the wrinkles in her cotton pants and pulled the door open. There was the same gaze that was set on her through the glass, except now deep brown eyes were fixed on her from well above her height.

One huge hand extended towards her.

"Miss Rowe? I'm David Blake. The security company sent me over to escort you to the house."

"Please, call me Ehvah." Ehvah extended her own hand.

His handshake was firm, but it was obvious he used a tiny portion of his strength. She stood aside for him to enter.

"I'm afraid I haven't finished packing."

The foyer wasn't small, but his frame filled the area. Ehvah closed the door and took a few steps back in order to put some space between them.

"I was advised that you wouldn't have any luggage."

"My aunt said she would send someone over to do it, but I thought I would make a start."

No doubt Mara had a team of on-set minions at her disposal.

David scanned the room as he spoke.

"The car we brought has limited storage space. If it's possible to leave the luggage for a later transfer, it will be a much more comfortable ride for you."

He removed the black sunglasses that sat on the top of his spiky short dark hair. The style reminded her of a U.S. Marine.

"Sure, we can do that. Just let me grab a few things." She picked up her handbag from the foyer table and moved into the bedroom to retrieve her journal.

A cell ringtone sounded in the foyer and she heard David answer.

"Yes, I'm there now. No, she's leaving the luggage. We'll be on our way in five minutes. Yes, I understand."

Ehvah paused to listen, but he had ended the call. His last comment intrigued her. What was it he had to understand?

CHAPTER 7

Mara tilted her head to balance the cell phone between ear and shoulder, while untying the laces of her period costume boots.

"Do you have it?"

"No, nothing. Not one lead. I searched everything she left in the hotel room. I couldn't find her cell phone—she must have it with her."

Lyle's negativity rang out over the line.

"Did you go into her laptop like I told you?"

"Of course I did. I even traced her internet history, and looked into every one of her contacts. Nothing stood out. She hasn't gone anywhere different, or messaged anyone we don't know. She's even given up contacting her new agent in the last month."

Mara sighed. She had been hoping this would be the end of it, that they would find what they were looking for.

"James had to have left me a clue. Hold on, I'll have another look at the letter."

She reached over the trailer table to grab her briefcase handle. The hairpiece pinned atop her head flopped over her forehead, impairing both her vision and her reach.

"Stupid." She pulled open the fastening clip and ripped it out.

"I'm doing my best, Mara. I don't have a whole lot to go on, and I have to do it all myself."

"I'm not talking to you, fool. The design team on this shoot is pathetic. If it was any other director, I'd walk off set." She spun the briefcase around to open it.

"Okay."

"Why did this trouble have to come just when I have a chance for a comeback! If you'd done what you were told, I wouldn't be dealing with this right now. James and I set up this money laundering scheme to be foolproof. Involving you was our only mistake."

"I told you I was sorry. The money I withdrew was a deposit for a vacation for the two of us. How was I to know they were monitoring the account?"

"Of course they were monitoring the account. What do you think Russian organized crime syndicates do with their dirty money? They might be using us to launder it, but that doesn't mean they trust us."

Mara peeked out the window to ensure there were no crewmembers close to the trailer.

"If you hadn't made that withdrawal, they wouldn't have known about our access to the money. James wouldn't be dead. We'd be sitting pretty on a fortune."

Mara flicked the combination to the briefcase.

"I had to watch my mother's acting career die. Then I had to watch her go from one man to another just to survive. She died worn out and poor. That is not going to happen to me. I finally have the chance for a career of my own, instead of being forced to live in the shadow of that girl."

"Isn't Ehvah like, twenty-four? She's hardly a girl." Lyle's desire for her niece was evident in his voice.

"She's nothing more than a two-bit sitcom actress. I got her career started, so I took from her what was mine."

Mara knew it wasn't true. Ehvah's major career moves had been made by her agent. He had steered every lucrative deal. Thankfully, she had managed to hang onto the lifestyle her niece afforded her.

Every chance she had of being somebody was dwindling. Thanks to Lyle's sloppy withdrawal, James was dead, and the money they had skimmed off the top of the laundering operation was sitting in an account they couldn't locate.

True to form, Lyle turned on the charm.

"Baby, you know you're the only one for me. I'd do anything for you, you know that."

"Oh, shut up and let me read this letter. Maybe there's something we missed."

Mara pulled the envelope out of the secret compartment at the back of the case.

It had been a shock when the letter had arrived yesterday. James's scrawl on the envelope had sent a chill up her spine. It had been over three weeks since his murder. The letter must have been lost in the system.

The letterhead showed the shelf company they had set up to exact their plan, the same company the FBI was now investigating.

She read the contents to herself.

My Love,

I am sending you this information the old-fashioned way so it can't be traced or overheard. I just had a visit from two FBI agents. They have picked up on a suspicious account withdrawal. I assured them it wasn't us, but I don't know who made it. Have you divulged our plan to anyone else? I suspect Lyle. If so, he has made a very bad mistake. We must pull back and reassess future withdrawals before proceeding. I am now certain the FBI have been monitoring me.

If the FBI knows of this withdrawal, I am concerned others will know also. I will try to negotiate our way out of this mess.

To be safe, I have transferred the money out of the US account to a more secure location.

Yours always, James.

PS: If something should happen to me, Ehvah has the account details although she doesn't know it.

Mara shook her head. If only he had gone into more detail about the location of the money, or where he had planted the details.

"It says Ehvah has the account details. Nothing more. It's got to be in her belongings. Did you get everything out of her hotel room?"

"Everything she has here in Australia."

"Well, you'll have to go back to the States and go through everything there as well. The FBI has cleaned out the office, but it could be in her room somewhere. And check her car."

Mara pulled off her boots and massaged her toes. *Someone should be here doing this for me.*

"You don't think she knows where it is?" Lyle asked.

"Not a chance. She never took an interest in business. Not that she trusted me. Why do you think I kept James around as long as I did? He was the one she trusted. Unfortunately for her, he loved me more." Ehvah would have kicked Mara out along ago if James hadn't been hiding her spending, and then her money-making scheme.

"She's smart. She could figure things out, or she might come across the information by accident."

Lyle made a good point. "I know, so we have to watch her and make sure she's in no state to think. Did you switch those pills like I told you to?"

"Yeah. I don't think she'll notice."

"Good. That should keep her quiet for a while. I've got the security in place to watch her, and those tablets will put her out of action. I'm having her watched round the clock, so if she makes a move we'll know about it. In the meantime, get back home and do a search."

Mara rubbed at a wrinkle on her forehead. The director had insisted she stop using Botox fillers for months before the shoot. He wanted her to look as natural as possible.

"This humidity is unbearable."

"You're sensational, darling." Lyle had his sweetest voice on, still trying to pacify her from his previous slight.

Mara smiled. At forty-nine, her looks might be fading, but she had managed to stave off the ravages of time thanks to Ehvah's money. She looked like her mother did in her prime—beautiful, dark, and alluring. She and Ehvah's mother, her half-sister, may have shared the same famous father, but Mara was an aspiring actress who had never made it to the big time. Her sister was a musician with a husband who adored her. They were the most successful husband-and-wife team in the music industry. Until their tragic deaths.

And then I ended up with everything.

She took out a compact and stared into it.
"I am sensational. And I intend to stay that way."

CHAPTER 8

David Blake's head thumped in sequence with the bass beat reverberating around the veranda. His client was on a bender, and it was doing his head in.

He looked out to the flawless view of sand, sea, palm trees, and tropical splendor.

"Suffering in paradise," he murmured to himself, and stretched out on the timber railing. "Lord, give me strength."

He checked his cell phone for service. The signal levels showed one bar. It was the one disadvantage to Millionaire's Row. It amazed him that the elite could erect such expensive, lavish houses but neglect to address the lack of cellular service.

David squeezed his eyes shut as the other occupant in the house let out a loud "Yeah, Yeah, Yeah," that was easily heard over the stereo. Ehvah Rowe was living up to her reputation as good girl gone wild.

His ringtone sounded, barely audible above the noise. The caller ID showed it was his boss at the security company where he was contracted.

He answered with a simple, "Blake."

"How's things at celebrity central? Has she settled down?"

"Does this sound like settled down?" David held the phone in the direction of the veranda door.

"Sorry, Dave. I had no idea she was such a handful. I appreciate you taking this job. I don't have anyone else on the books who could have done the hours."

What his boss meant was that, other than him, he had no staff without family or responsibilities. The hours were long, but at least the money was good.

"Is she completely out of control? I can send Boof over to give you a break, if you want."

David looked back to the house, contemplating the escape his boss offered.

"No, she's loud, but not hard work. Just send Boof over at eleven like yesterday."

There was no point subjecting his nightshift relief partner to the noise. Their charge had played out the same routine the day before, rising long after his seven am start, moping around the house watching television, and then playing loud music until she crashed at six.

David hadn't seen her eat anything. No wonder she was so thin.

"Alright. If I can spare Boof, I'll get him over a little earlier tonight."

David rubbed a hand over his throbbing forehead.

"Can you send him with some aspirin and a set of ear plugs?"

His boss laughed before the line went dead.

David secured the cell in his pocket and lifted his face to the light breeze filtering through the manicured gardens. This was a beautiful spot, even if he was having trouble enjoying it.

Millionaire's Row was located on a small section of coastline not far from the city. A handful of architecturally designed homes dotted the mountainous rainforest. It was accessible by one road that climbed a range and crossed a water channel. Nature had provided the perfect secluded location. Super-tight security added to this haven for the rich and famous.

The area saw a steady stream of celebrities come and go. This wasn't the first time David had been employed to work here, but this was his first live-in position. The job included temporary residence in the servant's quarters adjoining the main house.

The Queenslander style semi-mansion was the oldest in Millionaire's Row, but previous jobs had proven that it was by far the best. A wide veranda wrapped around the two sides of the house and enjoyed the beach view. The back end was secured by a natural edifice—a steep mountain face. The interior housed a sweeping open plan kitchen/dining/lounge area, all looking out towards the veranda. Behind this were five bedrooms, each with their own bathroom. The side veranda overlooked a lap pool running the length of the house.

The property boasted a prime hillside view. A rainforest collage of green covered the downward slope from the veranda steps to the beach below.

David had spent the majority of the last two days looking out over the green mass. The veranda was the best vantage point for security. If any paparazzi were going to find his client, they would have to come up that slope. His brief was to provide Ehvah Rowe with the highest security.

To date, the only intruders had been of the avian variety. That morning a flock of black cockatoos had taken up residence in the trees lining the foreshore. Their obnoxious squawks sounded above the beat of the music as the flock followed their leader to a tree close by. David stared at the vibrant array of colors splaying under each bird's tail. Some were deep red, almost burgundy. Others were a perfect balance of orange and yellow.

Two birds left the flock to swoop down and land on the grassy area short of the edge of the veranda.

From his elevated position he could see them peck at the dropped fruit beyond.

"What do you guys think of all this?" he asked them.

He was answered with a high pitched squawk.

David smiled. "Yeah, me too, mate."

The interior of the house went silent. Ehvah had turned off the music. David anticipated the next onslaught of violent noise, but it didn't come.

"What are they eating?"

The American-accented voice came from behind him.

David glanced back to see his charge standing in the door way peering over his shoulder at the birds. Her long blonde hair was pulled back in a ponytail, but still managed to look a ball of knots.

She was wearing the same pajama pants and singlet top she had worn the day before. The pants were oversize and baggy on her thin frame. The top, a dull yellow, served to highlight the shadows under her gaunt cheekbones. Her eyes looked huge—although that could be because her face was so thin.

He had seen a few photos of Ehvah Rowe. She was undeniably striking. Not pretty, but captivating. He didn't know a lot about her celebrity life—he'd been long past the teenybopper phase when her fame had been in its prime. Besides, he had never been interested in the lifestyles of the rich and famous. He had been told his indifference was what made him good at his job.

He compared the girl before him to the pictures he had seen. This girl was one hot mess. She took a few steps onto the timber decking to get a better look at the cockatoos. David pointed to the palms above.

"You see that tree up there? It drops those little nuts. The cockatoos love them."

She moved out to stand beside him.

"They're so pretty. And loud." The corners of her mouth turned up. "Loud enough to get over the stereo, anyway."

David let out a huff and positioned one foot on the lower rail. The huffing must have been louder than he had planned because she glared at him.

"Don't like my music?" One raised eyebrow challenged him.

David thought over his response. These celebrity types were often easily offended. After a few seconds of trying to string together positive words in his head, he decided to go with a gentle, but honest response.

"It's not my thing."

She smiled, and looked back down at the birds.

"You know what? It's not mine either." She tilted one corner of her mouth. "It is distracting, though."

It felt like she was acknowledging his presence for the first time since they had arrived at the house. In the security business he was accustomed to blending into the background and remaining invisible. This particular job was different, because it was around the clock. It had crossed his mind that if he clashed with the girl, it would be much harder to put in the hours.

David noticed her enormous eyes were the most vibrant green he had ever seen. Strikingly green, with flecks of gold and a thin grey haze drifting across them. The dullness defined a person under medication. He had seen it often enough in his line of work to recognize the symptom.

Her eyelids drooped and she reached up to rub her face.

"I need some distractions. Nothing like a loud screaming noise to distract you. Right?"

"I suppose." David licked his lips.

"I don't know." She stopped to bend her back into a stretch. "Loud music seemed to work yesterday, but today it's doing my head in."

David couldn't help but laugh. It was exactly how he was feeling.

"I guess there's a reason why they call it heavy metal. 'Cause it feels like you've been bashed over the head with a lump of heavy metal if you listen to it for too long." She rolled her droopy eyes.

David noticed a slur in her voice accompanying her lack of awareness and drowsy demeanor. He thought back to when he had collected her at the hotel. He hadn't detected any sign of medication in her behaviour then. This version of her had surfaced the morning after they had arrived.

She slumped down onto the rail and rested her chin in her hands.

They looked out at the view for a few minutes, listening to the crash of the waves on the shore below and the conversational squawking of the cockatoos.

David glanced over to make sure she wasn't drifting asleep when she broke the silence.

"Have you ever seen anyone who's died? Like a dead body?"

His boss had filled him in on her background, why she was there, and the recent situation she had found herself in back home. He had caught a news report on the murder of her uncle as well. He knew enough about shock to see she wasn't coping well.

Real pity for her stirred in his stomach. Normally he wouldn't indulge in deep and meaningful conversations with his clients, but this girl didn't seem to have any help coming her way. She was all alone, and he had been told that she would have no visitors.

Lord, what can I say to help her?

The honest, but cautious route had served him well on her last question. He may as well apply that tactic again.

"Yeah, I've seen a few dead people."

"What's a few? Like two, three?"

"I was in the army, so I've seen a lot of death."

Even though it was a simple fact, it sounded cold to his ears. Almost flippant. It wasn't.

She raised her eyebrows. "Anyone you knew?"

"Too many people I knew. And too many I didn't."

"That sucks." She chewed on her thumbnail. "Did it affect you? I'm not trying to pry into your life or anything—it's just I'm kind of freaked out by what happened with my uncle. Is it natural to be this stressed?"

David thought for a moment before answering. "Yes, it's natural."

"So did you get stressed when you were in the army? Or do they train you not to be?"

"I was trained to handle all aspects of combat, including the stress that goes with it, but it affects everyone differently. Some people handle it better than others."

He paused to shift the weight of his stance. He racked his brain for further words of wisdom.

"Some think they're dealing with it at the time, but then it comes out years later. Every person handles trauma in their own way. There's no perfect cure, but some ways are probably healthier than others."

She tilted her head, the knotted mass of the ponytail dropping over one shoulder.

"So what are the healthy ways?"

David moved his foot off the bottom rail and took a deep breath. He hadn't anticipated becoming a therapist. For one, he didn't have any training in the field, and second, he wasn't the person to ask. He had just worked through that particular problem himself.

An idea occurred to him. "Well, talking about it helps. Maybe you need some professional advice." He thought he could at least try and point her in the right direction.

"I went to some trauma specialist back home. He gave me sleeping pills, but I think they're making me feel worse. I'll show you."

She took off back into the house.

David slapped his hand onto the railing.

Great. Just great. Now she thinks you're some sort of expert.

He shook his head and mentally kicked himself for getting involved.

"Here."

She held a bottle out to him as she stumbled through the doorway.

David grabbed her outstretched hand, righting her before she fell. The bottle transferred to him as he secured her to the rail.

"I'm not an expert. If you're unhappy with your care, you need to see a professional."

He glanced at the bottle. The tranquilizer was strong, but the dosage was small. Either she was taking way more than she needed, or she was having some sort of reaction to them.

"Are you taking the prescribed amount?"

"I only take them when I can't sleep, but in the last few days they're starting to make me feel weird, like I don't know what day it is, or even what time."

David held out the bottle for her to take back.

"What should I do about it?" She looked at the label. With her shoulders slumped, and head down, she looked about as hopeless as a person got.

Argh.

The inward groan reverberated thorough him. He thought back to a time when he needed help. He had to do something.

"Look, I know someone. Ron. He's a friend of mine, a psychologist. I've known him and his family since I was a kid. If you like, I could find out if he'll visit you here. Maybe he can help you? Check out the prescription at least?"

She peered up from under her lids. Big green eyes fixed on him while her lips twitched.

"Sure. That sounds great."

David retrieved his phone from his pocket.

CHAPTER 9

Ehvah took a deep drink of water and placed the empty glass back on the table.

"I think I'm starting to understand my actions better. My choices in life since my family died. It's all making a lot more sense. And I'm not having the nightmares as often, so that's good."

"That's great." Ron Murray lifted one leg to cross the other. "Understanding is sometimes the first step to forgiveness and love. The conscious act of internal analysis—that is, looking inside ourselves and analyzing our actions, thoughts, and feelings—is paramount to a happy life."

Ehvah nodded.

"How are you enjoying being here?" He smiled, an infectious grin filling his face.

"It's amazing. I love it."

Ehvah sighed deep, and absorbed the superior coastal view framed by the glass doors. It felt as though the Millionaire's Row house had cast some sort of spell on her. The calmness she felt here was addictive.

"How about the isolation? Not feeling lonely?"

She considered Dr. Murray's question.

"No. It's funny, but I've never felt lonelier than when I was doing television, and singing. I was in the middle of a fame spike, surrounded by people, and I felt so lonely. Here there's just two of us most of the time, and I haven't felt lonely once."

She and David hadn't had a lot of deep and meaningful conversations, but there was something natural and easy about his presence. She found herself seeking out his company, not because she desired his attention, but because his presence evoked a heightened sense of reassurance within her.

"Dave's a great bloke. I've known him a long time. He's a big strong man. You're in safe hands."

For some reason, Dr. Murray's statement inspired a flash vision of her security man's thick torso and oversized hands. The mental picture triggered a hot flush that started in her chest and travelled up her neck and into her cheeks. She picked up her empty glass and ran one finger around the rim.

"He seems like a nice guy."

"You and he have a lot more in common than you think."

Dr. Murray lifted one eyebrow along with the corner of his mouth.

His cryptic statement inspired another warm flush, along with a desire to find out more about her security man.

***

David took one last look around the perimeter of the house before settling back into his position on the veranda. He had been here exactly three weeks, and in that time life had been uneventful.

Apart from him and Ehvah, the only other visitors were Boof, his security night relief, and his psychologist friend, Dr. Ron Murray, who visited Ehvah every second day. The murmur of voices coming from inside the house signaled the end of the doctor's session.

David addressed him as he stepped out onto the veranda. Ehvah was nowhere in sight.

"How's it going?" David had managed to avoid personal conversations with the girl since Ron had started visiting. But it was clear the sessions were having a remarkable effect.

"She's going to be okay." Ron set his old leather briefcase down at the door and made his way over to stand at the edge of the decking.

Although he was a professional man, Ron Murray's casual attire favored his traditional islander heritage rather than his city slicker profession. His fuzzy mop of grey-tinged black hair was neat, but bordering on afro proportions, while his Hawaiian shirt blew in the ocean breeze. Dress shorts and loafers completed his tropical outfit.

"She's like anyone who's gone through a traumatic experience. She needs time." He flashed a white-toothed smile. "You know healing is an individual thing."

"Seems like she's on the road to recovery."

"She is better." Ron rubbed his forehead. "And she has a fighting spirit that will see her through. One of the first things I did was replace her medication. I couldn't understand why she was having such a negative reaction to it. It was nothing but a sleeping aid."

Ron paused to check back into the house before leaning towards him.

"Just between us?"

David nodded in confirmation.

"There's a chance her drugs were tampered with. The pills in the bottle were different to the prescription. It was filled in the States, so we can't rule out a pharmaceutical error, but it's strange. I'm only telling you because you need to keep an eye out for any suspicious visitors."

"That explains her being so out of it for the first few days, but no one's been here." David frowned. "There have been a few helicopters floating around, but they must have been local traffic."

When a helicopter had circled the house several times a week ago, David had assumed the paparazzi or a reporter had found Ehvah, but they hadn't stayed for long before leaving the airspace.

Ron rested his forearms on the rail. "How much does she communicate with you?"

David reached down to join him. "A lot more lately. She asks a lot of questions."

"About?" Ron raised his eyebrows.

"Mostly the country, and the wildlife." David recalled several conversations they had about the area, and the native flora and fauna.

Ron tilted his head, sending his afro bouncing.

"She hasn't mentioned her family?"

"Not much." David shook his head. "She did tell me she didn't trust her aunt. I haven't met her, but the boss and Boof tell me she's a real piece of work."

"I suspect that assessment is entirely accurate."

Ron moved off the rail, stood, and stepped back to the door to retrieve his case. "Behind all the bravado she's a real sweet girl."

David raised his eyebrows in disbelief.

Ron gave him a piercing look before continuing. "She could do with a friend. Especially one who knows a bit about what she's going through."

David took a deep breath and broke eye contact. There was no doubt Ron was asking him to go beyond the professional boundaries and make a personal effort with this girl. It wasn't that he didn't want to help her, but how could he do that without breaching protocol?

Ron came up behind him and slapped a hand on his shoulder.

"Just do me a personal favor and promise me you'll reach out to her a bit, hey?"

"I promise." After all this man had done for him, how could he not comply with his request?

***

Mara shooed the make-up woman away from her face.

"Do you mind? I have to take this call."

She didn't wait for the woman's answer before grabbing her cell phone off the table and leaving the set trailer. She slammed the door behind her before talking to Lyle.

"Are they still there?"

"Yeah. I can't get near the place."

Mara knotted the tie of her robe and moved away from the door into a more private corner of the parking lot.

"You have to find a way to get into the house. You've been in L.A. for three weeks. What are you doing?"

"It's impossible. The FBI have a man stationed there twenty-four-seven."

"Are they in the house?"

47

"No. Outside."

Mara rolled her eyes at Lyle's incompetence.

"Well, find a door they aren't monitoring and get in there. Did your criminal family teach you nothing?"

There was a slight pause on the line before Lyle answered. "I may need their help."

Mara groaned, then walked several more feet away from the trailer so she wouldn't be overheard.

"Lyle, do not involve your family. Do you hear me? Now, get into that house and turn it upside down. The information we need has to be in there. I'd do it myself, but I'm stuck here. Don't blow this."

"Is Ehvah still down in the beach house?"

Mara rubbed a hand over one throbbing eye, not caring a whit about the last hour she had spent in the make-up trailer.

"Yes. The security firm tells me she hasn't gone out. She hasn't had any visitors, except some shrink she's employed. I don't know if she's still taking the tablets. This security company is far too vague with their reports, but it's too late to change them now."

"I'll do everything I can to get into the house, my love."

Mara rolled her eyes. "You'd better."

***

David acknowledged Ehvah as she stepped out onto the veranda.

She had spent most afternoons outside in his presence, either writing in a journal or reading a book Ron had left for her. David recognized the title. He had read the same book when he was in need of some direction. He had smiled when he'd first seen her with it, and wondered if it would have the same effect on her as it had on him. Reading it had led him to another book, a book which changed his life.

She settled onto the day bed at the far end of the veranda to read. Her appearance had changed from when they had first arrived. The pajamas had gone, and she dressed every morning. Her hair was still brittle and straw-like, but at least it looked clean, pulled back in a plait. And she was eating more. It had surprised him when she had suggested they take turns preparing meals. Some days, when neither felt like cooking, they would just pick over the food Boof brought over each night.

Having a client who sought out his company was a new experience for David. The people he worked for preferred him to be in the background of their lives. He had to admit that he enjoyed her company as well. She didn't talk a lot, but was animated and interesting when she did. Some of her comments had made him think. She was young, but he had detected an old soul behind her eyes.

He watched her profile with interest. She wore glasses for reading, and the frames complimented her face.

David enjoyed her parent's music. A number of their songs were classics. Ehvah looked a little like her mother. Maybe it was the combination of intelligence and striking features, but he found it hard to keep his eyes off her at times.

There was an edginess about her that he suspected could turn wild if she was crossed. But he had detected a naturally endearing sweetness that balanced this out. She was a complex person with many layers.

A scuttling noise sounded at the garden's perimeter. A goanna was making its way up a gum tree. The oversize lizard stopped mid-climb to poke out its forked tongue, smelling the air in search of prey. David could see the creature's claws clinging to the bark, while its body hung rigid in a horizontal position against the trunk. A sudden flurry of wings burst from the branches of the tree, revealing that the creature's prey had become aware of its stalker.

"What is that thing?" Ehvah was up and off the daybed in one swift motion.

"It's a goanna. Big lizard," he answered.

"That is the meanest looking creature I have ever seen." Her eyes widened with wonder.

"They're formidable characters. They'll eat just about anything." David walked the length of the veranda to stand near her.

"I hope that doesn't include us."

"No, but you don't want to be standing near one when it's looking to run. They'll take off up the nearest tall object, including a human leg."

She gave him a look of open-mouthed horror.

"What do you do if that happens?"

"Holler like mad, I guess."

Her laughter was a sweet sound. She ran her hand up and down the weathered timber railing. A lingering silence fell, and David frowned at the tension it generated in the air.

Ehvah shuffled her feet a little, rubbed the back of her neck, then crossed and uncrossed her arms.

"I've been wanting to say that I'm sorry I was a bit out of it when we first arrived. I kind of accosted you. It wasn't me, you know. I had the wrong medication."

David decided not to tell her he knew about the mix-up.

"It's all good. You seem much happier."

"I am, thanks. You were right. Talking about it helps a lot."

He motioned to the book lying on the bed.

"What do you think of that?"

"The book?"

He nodded.

"It's amazing. I'm on my third read-through."

"Wow, I only got through it once. You must be a fast reader."

She smiled. "Only when it's something that interests me. What did you think of it?"

David took a deep breath, remembering his promise to reach out to her.

"It was the beginning of something that changed my life."

Ehvah bit her bottom lip.

"I think it may be doing that for me. I never looked at things the way this author does. Like the concept that worrying won't add a moment to your life."

David tilted his head, encouraging her to continue.

"I hear clichéd catchphrases like that all the time, but I've never thought to put it into the perspective of my own fears. It's so true that every day has already been assigned to you, so worrying about tomorrow is useless energy." She shrugged slim shoulders. "It takes away from living the moment you have. It's freeing when you genuinely embrace it."

"That's not an easy concept to accept. So many people have an intense fear of death, and do everything they can to avoid it. But ultimately, it's a timeline that's out of our hands."

"True." She raised her eyebrows, causing a thin crease to appear on her forehead. "None of us controlled our birth, so how can any of us control our death? It makes sense when you think about it. What's the use of fearing every single thing, and analyzing every negative scenario to the point of paralysis of your life when ultimately you have no control over it?"

She looked out to the garden beyond. "The only control you have is over the way you live. The how, not the beginning, or the end, only the in between."

David kept his attention on her as she spoke. She had a much better grip on the themes of the book than he had. It had taken him some time to get to the same point. She was more mature than he'd thought. How much younger than him was she? He did the mental math. Six years.

"Sorry, I overshared. You could say it's made an impact on me."

The math strain must have shown on his face, because she swallowed hard and moved away to pick up the book.

David took a step towards her, sorry that he hadn't reinforced his personal approval for her statement.

"Hey, I agree with you. I reckon that's a great take on it."

She looked back at him as she stepped through the doorway. For a moment her eyes met his. Gold flecks in vibrant green glistened.

"Thanks."

She disappeared into the house.

CHAPTER 10

The sun felt like it was burning laser beams into her skin. Ehvah angled her back in order to get the full effect. After weeks of soaking up the tropical Australian sun, she still marveled at just how hot it was. The same star that shone over the entire planet felt like a foreign force in this country. Even with the added humidity driving its intensity, it was a comforting feeling to be encased in its energy.

Ehvah closed her eyes and concentrated on the feeling of her skin tightening, the sound of the lapping waves below the house as they collided with the shore, the soft turf of the groomed lawn under her beach towel, the reflections of light shining off the lap pool just meters away, and the never-ending chatter of the native birds around her.

Yep—Australia is just what I need.

There was no denying the serenity of the place.

Peace. I need peace.

The realization made her sit up and smile. Dr. Murray's visits had had an effect on her.

New medication meant she was sleeping better, and the therapy sessions were unravelling the emotional mess of her teenage years. Now, if she could just forget James's death and the snake tattoo, she would have a chance at getting her life back on track.

Unfortunately, the occasional nightmare forced her into the reality of what she had seen.

What am I going to do?

The question was forefront in her mind. She had to do something, but what? She didn't have the strength to take on a murderer.

Ehvah grabbed her phone and checked her social media status. She had refrained from posting any updates since James's death, but speculation surrounding the case, and her disappearance from public view had sparked a flurry of activity on her sites.

Most of the comments were positive—fans reaching out to her and asking if she was okay. There were the usual nasty remarks from internet trolls, mostly regarding tabloid photos of her in various clubs. The trashy magazines loved a good girl gone bad story and would periodically feature her, especially if the paparazzi photos were exceptionally unflattering ones.

For the most part, the entertainment world ignored her. She'd had her day and was old news. Well, unless she entered a rehab clinic—then they would say how sad it was that she needed help, or if she died of an overdose, then they would mourn her as they did all tragic former stars. The mourning period would last a full week if she were lucky. They might even say how perfect it was that she had gone to be with her equally tragic parents.

Ugh.

The thought enflamed a heavy indignation within, and she threw her phone down on the towel.

She looked up to the veranda, conscious of the fact that she wasn't alone. David was seated on one of the outdoor chairs, far enough away to give her some space, but close enough to be a watchful presence.

Since Dr. Murray's last visit, and following their conversation about him, Ehvah had felt herself transitioning from relying on David's strength of presence to suddenly being highly attuned to his presence.

Dr. Murray was right about his strength. His chiseled body reminded her of a superhero. His dark, rugged features and deep chocolate-brown eyes possessed a raw magnetism. But there was a lot more to this man than physical prowess. Ehvah found her desire to know more about him increasing daily. Unfortunately, they weren't at that personal questioning stage, and Ehvah had no idea how to move the relationship from friendly camaraderie into a more intimate arena.

She pulled her legs to her chest and watched a flock of strange birds strut their way over the long stretch of green grass in front of her. David had told her they were called white ibis. Their long black beaks jutted out as the procession moved along, pecking at the grass.

It felt good to sit and admire the birds, to get away from humanity, to almost disappear from human view. How was the world viewing her?

Her curiosity piqued, and she retrieved her phone and Googled her name. She scrolled down the matches. The usual tabloid fodder she attracted loaded, accompanied by a few new posts.

Pop Princess Ehvah Rowe Flees to Australia.

So much for a graceful exit.

Ehvah Seeks Help to Deal with Stepfather's Murder.

Slightly accurate at least.

Rehab for Drug Problems—Ehvah Rowe Admitted.

WHAT! Stupid. She hit page two and waited for the screen to refresh.

"I saw nothing." Ehvah Rowe admits to being in the house when her stepfather was murdered.

She closed the device and threw it back down.

The clunking of the veranda door signaled Boof's arrival at the house.

Ehvah had learned that Boof and Ron Murray were related. It wasn't hard to pick the family resemblance in the native features, but there was a great divide between the two men when it came to size. Boof was taller than his older cousin and much wider. Ehvah shuddered to think of the weight he would have behind him should he have to use it. For all his bulk, Boof had a childlike grin, a happy demeanor, and a giggle that never failed to make her laugh.

The big islander man checked in to relieve David well after sundown each evening. He was early tonight.

He gave her a thumbs-up, and a big grin over the short distance between them. She returned a wave. David stood with his hands in the pockets of his shorts, lips curved up at the ends, looking at her in some sort of secret amusement.

Ehvah removed her sunglasses, and their eyes connected for a split second before she pretended to be busy with her phone again. She fiddled with the settings for a while before a thought prompted her to open the internet browser again.

David Blake Australia.

The search engine swung into action.

The first page was a dead loss. Not one match. She was about to click on the second page when a shadow fell across her towel.

"Do you mind if I take a swim?"

She looked up to find David standing over her. He was wearing nothing but a pair of board shorts. A towel rested over his bare shoulder. She panicked, throwing the phone down before he could see what she was doing.

"Sure." Ehvah indicated behind her to the lap pool. "The water's a bit cool. I went in for a dip earlier."

"I might not be in too long then."

His lips parted to reveal one slightly crooked tooth. Some may have considered it to be a blemish in an otherwise chiseled face, but Ehvah had decided that it added character. There was an accompanying scar just under his jawline. It stood out from her vantage point. She had wondered more than once what caused it.

You are taking far too much notice of this guy.

"How did you get the scar?"

The question was out of her mouth before she could stop it.

What are you thinking?

David must have wondered the same thing, because his eyebrows raised and his smile broadened.

"You really want to know?"

Yes, yes I do.

She didn't dare say the words out loud.

He placed one hand on top of the towel, repositioning it on his shoulder. The movement prompted a fluid ripple through his muscular torso.

For a second Ehvah's mortification was replaced by a distinct pang of desire.

"Um, yeah, sure."

Cool. Not.

David screwed up one side of his mouth.

"It's a bit of an embarrassing story. Not all that interesting, either."

"Go on, tell her," Boof called from the veranda. He was evidently enjoying the moment.

David shook his head.

"He was riding in a paddock and . . ." Boof hollered from his vantage point.

"Boof!" David swung back at him.

"What? I was there, remember?"

Ehvah sat up and crossed her legs. Maybe Boof could tell her what Google couldn't.

"How could I forget?" David rolled his eyes.

"So he's on this chook chaser, right . . ." Boof continued his story.

"Chook chaser?" Ehvah required further explanation.

"Oh, yeah, sorry. I forgot you don't know Aussie stuff." Boof made a high pitched whirring noise, similar to an obnoxiously loud trail bike. "That kind of bike's a chook chaser."

Ehvah smiled at his rendition, but nodded to indicate her understanding.

"So he's in this paddock. Nothing in it but one telephone pole. A group of girls walk by, so he pulls a wheelie."

Boof added some physical theatre to the story. His hands held imaginary motorbike handles, and his massive stance squatted in riding posture. The comic nature of the performance was not lost on Ehvah. She smiled as his body jiggled.

"So he's looking over at these chicks and runs right into the pole, stacks the bike, and is out cold." Boof exploded into a fit of laughter.

Ehvah couldn't help but join in. Boof's hilarity was infectious.

"Go on, have a good laugh. I can take it." David was smiling along with them. "At least I didn't fall into a long drop trying to impress a woman."

"Oh, no, you're not going to tell her about that." Boof's laughter ceased.

"Long drop? Is that a toilet?" Ehvah looked to David, who nodded.

Boof hightailed it into the house, raising a hand in disgust as he went. He clearly wasn't hanging around to find out if David was going to share his bathroom disaster tale.

"It's a bush toilet. Basically a hole in the ground. A really big, deep hole, full of really bad stuff. Do you know how hard it is to get a bloke the size of Boof out of something like that? It involved a crane and several towropes."

Ehvah was in fits of laughter again at the mental picture. "So you guys have known each other for a long time then?" she asked when she managed to catch her breath.

David took a seat on the grass next to her towel. "I spent my school holidays in the same community as Boof. My uncle owned fishing boats, and I'd come up from down south to help him out. But I didn't get this scar falling off the bike that time. The only thing I hurt then was my pride."

Ehvah admired his honesty.

"I got this," he stopped to touch the scar at his jawline, "when I ran into a barbed wire fence. That accident was a bit before the telephone pole incident. I rode my bike a bit hard there for a while."

David removed the beach towel from around his neck, unveiling a tattoo high on the back of his right shoulder. It was a crown of some sort, with a half-sun arch above it.

He placed the towel beside him.

"Now, I get to ask you something."

"Alright, I guess that's fair." Ehvah busied her hands by picking at grass strands.

"Why all the angst with the phone? I thought you were going to toss it into the pool at one point."

Ehvah picked up the phone. She looked at the darkened screen, knowing if she awoke the cell it would reveal that she had been searching his name. She placed it back down on the towel. Surely he didn't see it before.

"Um . . . nothing interesting. My social media sites didn't amuse me, and then I made the mistake of searching my name. I don't know how these people come up with this stuff. It's worse than lies—some of it is outright slander."

David leaned on his left side away from her.

"Cyberspace can be scary."

Ehvah shifted towards him.

"You got that right. I don't know why I bother with it."

"The way I see it, you can live there, or here. The power lies with you."

"What do you mean?" His comment intrigued her.

"I prefer to spend time in the real world. The cyber world can give you every detail about pretty much anything, but it won't give you one experience. It can show you places, things, relationships, it can tell you how to live, but it can never give you a life. It's unreal. This—" He swung his arm around and out to the ocean beyond. "This is real."

Ehvah saw his point. "You're right. This is a much better existence, but the internet isn't all evil. It's bad because of the horrible people that are in it."

"I didn't say that it was evil, just that it's not real. And there are no people on the internet, just personas. In the real world, people are people. In cyber world, a person isn't able to be anything but a persona."

She raised her eyebrows as he continued.

"Sure, some people choose to have a more honest or accurate persona than others, but unless you're physically with a person, you'll never get a completely honest impression as to who they are. I think a lot of people forget that."

Ehvah considered what he said. She had spent weeks with him, but still reverted to Googling his name.

"You can physically be with someone and not know as much about them as you would like." As soon as the words were out of her mouth a hot flush swamped her cheeks. She fidgeted with the seam of the towel in the hope of disguising her nervousness. He was going to know she was talking about him.

Ugh.

The inward cringe reverberated through her body. She peeked over to see David looking down at his wriggling toes.

"That's true, but you can also think you've worked someone out, and then they go and surprise you." He beamed a massive smile her way, then jumped to his feet and dived into the pool.

Was he talking about her as she was about him?

Ehvah watched his body forge a smooth path through the water, his back rippling with his powerful strokes.

Another tattoo sat on the top of his left shoulder blade. It was a black bird with a piercing yellow eye. It resembled a crow, but had white streaks on its wings. She cocked her head to the side to make out another winged symbol next to the bird with wording in the middle. *Who Dares Wins*.

Ehvah sat, mesmerized by the bird's fluid motion, until David turned.

Ugh.

The cringe reverberated again, this time in reaction to a hot flash of desire that ran through her.

CHAPTER 11

Ehvah smiled at Boof as she made her way through the lounge area with two steaming cups of coffee. He looked up from his cell phone to acknowledge her. He already had his morning brew. The retro novelty cup he preferred was sitting on the coffee table next to him, and he was in deep conversation with his boss. Ehvah could hear him recounting the details of the job he went to before arriving here each night.

She shook her head in personal amusement as she walked past him. He was propped up with several pillows at his back, one arm behind his head, and one foot on the coffee table next to his cup. The early morning sunlight flowed in from the open doorway and onto the seat next to him.

Most clients would have a fit if they saw their security man in that position, but Ehvah reveled in the casual atmosphere they had all fallen into. The easy camaraderie between them all felt friendly, secure and honest. It was a place she hadn't felt in a long time, and it was most likely why she hadn't ventured out, why she hadn't missed socializing.

She gripped the sliding glass door to the veranda with her toes and balanced the two coffees as it opened. It was unusual for her to be up this early, but she had woken fresh after a restful sleep and had decided to join the men rather than sit in her bedroom.

She had seen David reading a book outside and decided to take him a drink. Her heart missed a beat as he looked up and gave her a wide smile. His deep brown eyes held a warm greeting that triggered a second skip inside her chest.

"You're up early."

"I couldn't sleep any more."

As she placed her cup on the table between them, she saw the book he had been reading was the Bible.

"I didn't know you were religious."

It was a strange discovery. She couldn't recall anything he had said or done that linked him with a divine leaning.

David retrieved his cup.

"I'm not religious, but I do have a strong faith." He stopped to sip his drink. "I guess you could say I'm a follower of Jesus."

For a second Ehvah couldn't believe what he had said.

"You're kidding. That's the same thing my grandmother used to say—that she was a follower of Jesus. That's so weird that you would say that too." She shook her head at the coincidence. She hadn't heard anyone say that since her grandmother had passed.

"Were you close to her?"

"Gran looked after me right from when I was born. My parents had a faith of sorts as well. Not early in their career, but towards the end. Dad used to say that God was the final frontier in music. Gran was basically my nanny. She would read me Bible stories. We even recited verses."

David laughed as she recited a few verses in the sing-song tone of a child.

"It was hard when my parents died, but losing Gran was harder. That was the first time I felt like an orphan. Everyone had deserted me. I think I felt like God had too."

David reached over and picked up the book. He flipped through the pages before settling on one. "Can I read you something?"

"Sure." Ehvah attempted to tidy her unruly hair. She felt as though the connection between them had grown stronger with this discovery. It was a strange feeling, but knowing David and the people she had loved most in the world shared the same faith gave her an uncanny sense of coming home. That somehow they approved of him, or maybe even had sent him when she so desperately needed a friend.

His finger followed the words as he read.

"Therefore I tell you, do not worry about your life, what you will eat or drink; or about your body, what you will wear. Is not life more important than food, and the body more important than clothes? Look at the birds of the air; they do not sow or reap or store away in barns, and yet your heavenly Father feeds them. Are you not much more valuable than they? Who of you by worrying can add a single hour to his life? Do not worry about tomorrow, for tomorrow will worry about itself. Each day has enough trouble of its own."

He looked up at her.

"It's from Matthew. Remind you of anything?"

Ehvah knew straight away what he meant.

"The book Dr. Murray gave me."

"The author of that book is a Christian psychologist. He's taken the words of Jesus and used them. Ron's also a Christian psychologist. He's been a great help to me."

Ehvah took a deep breath and looked out to the rising sun on the ocean horizon.

"Dr. Murray told me that apart from his knowing you for a long time, you're also an old patient."

David placed the ribbon marker at the page and closed the Bible.

"I was in the service for most of my young adult life. I left two years ago." He gave her a tight-lipped smile. "Ron Murray diagnosed me with post-traumatic stress disorder. It's common among returned soldiers, but anyone who's suffered a traumatic event in their lives can have a bout of it."

"That must be why he told me you would understand what I was going through." Ehvah stared into her coffee.

"I can't say I'm any sort of expert, but I do know what it feels like to be going through it. I'm one of the lucky ones. I had Ron, and then my faith to see me through."

"How did your faith help?"

David wet his lips before speaking.

"My faith in Jesus taught me to give up trying to control

everything on my own. A lot of my PTSD was about my lack of control over what happened to those I loved."

"Were you afraid you'd die as well?"

"No, not afraid for myself. At first I had a lot of guilt about surviving. I can honestly say I wanted to die. When I overcame that fear, I became petrified of doing something that might cause someone else to die."

He stopped to rub the back of his neck.

"My journey there is a long story, but my faith taught me that the balance of life and death doesn't lie in my hands. That ultimately I'm not the orchestrator of either my destiny or anyone else's. God is. And He's fully invested in all our lives."

His deep brown eyes held a depth of emotion that Ehvah couldn't reach the bottom of. She broke away from his gaze.

Was God invested in her destiny? Even though she had given up trusting in Him?

David reached out to touch her arm, sending a shock wave through her entire body.

"But, hey, I don't have it all worked out. Each person diagnosed with PTSD has a different story, and different coping mechanisms. My faith is more than a fix for one problem. It's about submitting every part of my life to God. Even though I may not know where I'm heading day-to-day, it's a great feeling to know that He does."

Ehvah bit her bottom lip and thought about her parents. Their faith had come through in their lyrics about loving others and persevering through hard times. Although they had left the earth unexpectedly, they certainly left a lasting legacy of faith.

What legacy do you want me to leave, God?

Ehvah sat up straight. For the first time since she was a child, she realized she genuinely wanted to know what God thought.

A pair of large black and white birds flew close to the railing, breaking her thoughts. One let out an ear-piercing squawk while the other settled on the grass and warbled a disjointed tune. Their body shape and color reminded her of

David's inking.

"Is that the bird in your tattoo?"

She had asked the question before mentally filtering it for personal appropriateness.

David clearly didn't mind.

"What we have here is a pair of magpies. My tat is a currawong. They share a lot of similar traits. Both can put a big hole on your head if they decide to swoop, but the currawongs are a lot less aggressive towards humans than these guys."

"Are they aggressive towards other animals?"

"They can be. On my unit's first training mission we were out in the bush. Middle of nowhere . . ."

He paused to place a hand above his eyes to block the sunbeams showering through the palm trees.

" . . . we were all bunkered down in camouflage and this flock of currawongs comes swarming around us. They were so noisy. Not in a bad way, because they don't squawk like these guys, but there was a lot of them."

Ehvah smiled at the animated way he used his hands to explain the spectacle.

"It didn't take us long to work out that a pair of kookaburras had dropped in to drink at the waterhole nearby, and the currawongs decided the kookaburras didn't need to be there. They gang together to chase other birds out of their territory, and they're good at it. After that event, our unit adopted the currawong as a mascot."

"So who dares wins." Ehvah recalled the symbol close to the bird with words running down the middle.

"That's the motto of the unit I served with." David pulled up his t-shirt to reveal the other strange marking on his shoulder.

"This one's the Australian army insignia. It's called the rising sun. It's mostly worn as a badge on a slouch hat."

Ehvah nodded. "I've seen one of those hats. It's a cowboy hat with one side clipped up, right?"

David smiled at her. His eyes crinkled at the corners making her stomach do a flip-flop.

"That hat's called an akubra. It's standard issue for

Australian stockmen. The army's hat is called a slouch hat."
He ran a finger over the ink of the rising sun. "I had this
drawn here because of a story my great-grandfather used to
tell me."

Ehvah shaded her face so she could see him better.

"My great-grandfather served in World War Two in North
Africa. A place called Tobruk. The trench warfare was
severe, but the Aussies weren't there alone."

He paused to shift in his seat.

"One of the best fighting units in the world served beside
them, the Ghurkas. They were a combined elite fighting
group, mostly from Nepal. The Gurkhas would strip down to
a loincloth and wield a traditional knife that looked a little like
a curved machete. They would move silently through the
trenches in the pitch black of night."

David leaned into her. A whiff of his spicy deodorant
caught her senses.

"Granddad said the only sign you knew they were
behind you was a touch on the shoulder. They were feeling
for the rising sun badge the Australians would wear either on
their shoulder or on their collar. If they didn't feel it, they
assumed they were in contact with an enemy and slit the
throat."

He made a line across his neck.

"A Gurkha soldier would kill every enemy they could
reach. Imagine the Germans waking up to find several of
their soldier mates dead in the trench beside them. The
Gurkhas would also cut the ears off their victims. They
instilled a lot of fear in the enemy. I can imagine there were a
lot of sleepless Germans after an attack like that."

"Did they get caught?" Ehvah let out the breath she
didn't realize she had been holding.

"All the time. But they fought hard, and the only weapon
they needed was a traditional knife. The old man would say
that in the early days of the war, the rising sun saved him as
much as his own weapon did."

David shifted back in his seat.

"A tattoo of the rising sun on one shoulder is a bit of a
family tradition. My grandfather, Pop, has one too."

He picked up his coffee and peered at her over the rim. "So how does a celebrity get away with not having a tattoo these days?"

The cheeky flash in his eyes indicated he was teasing her. She reciprocated with her best effort. "Who says I don't have a tattoo?"

Wrinkles furrowed his brow. "It must be pretty well hidden if you can't see it in a swimsuit."

Ehvah's belly did a dive at the thought of him checking her out in her one-piece.

"Let's just say the one tattoo I have is close to my heart." She bit her bottom lip at the red flush forming on David's neck. "I got it in memory of my parents."

"My father's not a fan of the ink." David fidgeted with the mug handle. "He always says a tattoo is a permanent reminder of a temporary feeling. But for some of us, they can be reminders of those we care about. For others, I guess, they can be indications of hate or violence."

A flash of the snake's head trailing out of James's killer's neckline entered her head.

She knew she had to do something about it, but for now it was much easier to push that thought away and concentrate on the tropical view—and the man beside her.

***

"I told you, I'm not doing it."

Ehvah's voice echoed off the high ceiling. David shuffled further along the couch to get a fix on her position in the kitchen. He shouldn't have bothered, because she stormed into the dining area and grabbed an apple from the fruit bowl with one hand.

"Listen to me. No. N. O. I've said it before, and I'll say it again. I'm not your puppet, and I don't need the money."

David pulled back as she slammed the apple into the fruit basket. The bananas would be bruised.

"Fine with me. Good riddance."

She treated her cell phone with the same distain as the fruit. It buzzed as it hit the table. He met her fury with a shrug. She had been on the phone for ten minutes. He had no idea who the caller was, but they had stoked a fire inside her. He took some satisfaction in knowing that he wasn't wrong when he had discerned a fighting spirit underlying her attractive exterior.

"Can you believe the audacity of that man?" The gold flecks in her green eyes flashed. She didn't wait for him to answer. "He wanted me to do a tour of my old songs." She huffed, as if the concept was disgraceful.

"You don't want to do that?"

It seemed like a stupid question considering the spectacle, but David knew enough about women to know she was seeking his encouragement to continue.

"Why would I want to do a tour aimed at thirteen-year-old girls?" She waved her arms high. "My name is back in the media because I'm linked to an unsolved murder, and my agent wants to send me on a national children's tour—except my fans are as old as me, and most of them have moved on—like me. It would be a disaster."

As Ehvah sighed deep, David felt a sense of pity for her. Her life was in some sort of transition. She didn't fit into the world she used to belong to, and hadn't worked out her place in the future.

It's with you.

Excuse me?

The first thought flashed into his heart, the second into his head. No clear explanation was forthcoming. Ehvah didn't pick up on his inter-spiritual distraction.

"He told me he was done with me if I didn't do the tour. What was I supposed to do?"

She glared at him from across the wide timber table. One hand gripped the edge like a claw.

David forced his concentration back to the moment.

"It does seem like professional suicide."

"Huh. According to him, I've already committed suicide. I'm professionally dead, and I should be grateful that he's willing to take a chance on me. Like he's my savior or something!"

David felt a rise of indignation. This man had upset his client. He was the cause of her slumped shoulders, twitching jaw, clawed hand, dejected countenance, hurt demeanor, and pained expression.

Open your eyes.

The voice inside his head rang out again.

He admitted a sudden shift in his awareness of her since he had caught her Googling his name yesterday.

He had become far too curious about Ehvah Rowe even before seeing his name on her phone. Now, after having caught her in an intimate search for information on him, his attention was piqued. Why he found her so interesting was beyond his understanding.

All he knew was that no client had disturbed his solitary peace the way she had. It was unacceptable. His rising interest was driving him out of his depth. Now his imagination had switched into overdrive, conjuring up some sort of future with her.

He shook his head and formed a supportive reply.

"He sounds like a tool. You were right to sack him."

Green eyes flashed his way. "How dare you! I've never had any sort of physical relationship with my agent."

David was confused for a split second before he realized her misinterpretation of his Aussie slang.

"Sacked means to fire someone."

"Oh."

The pink haze on her cheeks cast a becoming shade across her face.

David felt one side of his mouth turn up, followed by an overwhelming desire to reach out and touch her. He averted his attention to his wriggling toes in order to gain some composure. He was reverting to this particular trick a lot.

"What are you going to do now? About your career?" He pulled himself up. It wasn't a question he would ask a client. The grip he had on his professional conduct had been dwindling away ever since he had made that promise to Ron to befriend her.

Ehvah sighed and rolled her neck. "I don't know."

She glanced eyes at him before fixing her gaze out to sea.

"Maybe I'll just stay here forever."

She looked back and cast a wide smile. With her hair piled on top of her head, hoop earrings, and floating hibiscus-print shift, she looked like a beach princess.

David could feel appreciation for her resonate through his body. Memories of her lounging by the pool entered his head and sent a heat wave through his body. He struggled to gain composure.

Get a grip. She's a client. You're here to do a job. Nothing more. Nothing less.

"Well, this is a great place." He squared his shoulders and moved at lightning speed to a safe position on the veranda.

Waves crashed on the foreshore below, and the wind whistled its melodic tune through palm leaves.

Clattering in the kitchen reminded him that his maddening distraction was close by. He knew his escape would be temporary.

So what if I am attracted to her. Nothing can be done about it. Even if something did happen, it would go nowhere. Stop being a fool and concentrate on doing your job.

It was the perfect internal brief—honest, and demanding strength and perseverance. David steeled himself to follow it—no matter what.

The ringing of his phone sent him reaching for the back pocket of his shorts.

He checked the caller I.D.

Ron Murray.

CHAPTER 12

Ehvah knew the pattern of this dream. Alone, helpless, fear, death, no escape. A curdled cry sounded in her throat, then another, and another.

A light burst through the darkness forcing her awake. She startled under the beam, her eyes registering shapes and contours. She wrapped her arms around her knees and tried to focus on something. The end of a bed came into view.

Where . . . ?

"Hey."

The male voice was soft and gentle beside her. She looked towards its source. Dark brown eyes held her own. Then a full head came into focus, along with a strong jawline, thick neck, and shoulders so broad that she shuddered at their strength.

She looked down to see a great hand splaying her shoulder.

David.

She released one hand from around her knees and rubbed her head. A vague realization of her surrounding pushed through the fuzz in her brain, along with a heavy swell of emotion. Rising tears threatened to overflow—then did.

"Hey, it's okay. It was just a dream."

She stretched her legs out as he pulled her to him and held her to his chest. She sucked back the tears.

"Settle now. You're okay."

Ehvah fell into his body, feeling a sense of connection she hadn't enjoyed in a long time. She became conscious of her breathing, shallow and labored. She concentrated on lengthening her intake and expulsion, discovering a new sensation in the earthy scent of his body.

She took a deep breath, uncurled her grip on his shirt, and focused on the bedroom. With gained control, she pulled away, rubbing her face in an effort to clear her head.

He kept a hand in the small of her back.

Ehvah took another deep breath, feeling a dry, sore patch at the base of her throat.

"I need some water."

She skimmed around his bulk to place her feet on the floor and headed for the kitchen where she switched on the light and retrieved a cup that sat upturned on the sink.

Ehvah could hear her rescuer enter the kitchen as she gulped down the tap water. She refilled the cup then turned to face him.

David leaned over a countertop. He was wearing loose sleeping clothes. Dark brown eyes fixed on her, and thick eyebrows deepened into a solid frown.

"Are you okay? You just about screamed the house down."

Ehvah scratched her scalp, feeling the knotting mass of her hair extensions. They were unbearable.

"I've been going without the sleeping pills. Five nights I've slept like a baby, then tonight . . ."

She was so disappointed. So many successful unmedicated nights had sparked hopes that the nightmares had gone.

"I'm sorry to have woken you."

"It's no problem." She managed a tight smile.

"I thought you were in trouble." He crossed his arms revealing the definition of his upper body though his t-shirt.

"No, just my crazy subconscious dumping a heap of anxiety in my lap." She sipped on the water.

David's frown deepened. "It was a major night terror. Do you have them often?"

She swallowed hard and moved to stand on the opposite side of the bench.

"I had bad nightmares when my parents and Gran died,

but I got busy with work and eventually they went away. This new wave came back just after James."

He looked down at his hands on the bench, then back up at her.

"It must have been a real hard time. I'm sorry you had to go through all that. You must miss your family."

Ehvah felt a flurry of warmth within. For some reason, hearing him say he was sorry had done something strange to her insides.

"Thank you. I do. It was hard. They were all I had, and we were really close. My Mom and Dad weren't career parents—they took me with them all the time. The only reason I wasn't with them when they died was because I had a horrible cold and Gran said I was better off staying behind. There were times, after Gran died, that I wished I'd been with them. I think that's when the nightmares started. But then I got super busy with a career of my own."

"You scared the living daylights out of me." One corner of his mouth turned up.

"I'm just keeping you on your toes, giving you security people something to do." Ehvah bit her lip.

David looked towards the veranda. "Speaking of security people, where's Boof?"

He covered the distance to the door. A stiff ocean wind swept through the house as he exited.

"Boof. Wake up, ya mug."

A heavy knocking sound followed. Ehvah shifted her weight to get a better look. The big man had gone to sleep on the daybed, and was now attempting to extract his oversized bulk out of the narrow space between the furniture and the railing.

Ehvah made her way back down the hallway. David would handle the slumbering Boof.

She took one of the mild sleeping pills Dr. Murray had prescribed and shuffled back into bed, leaving the door open and the bedside lamp on.

How embarrassing.

She shook her head at the thought of the scene. It was bad enough that David had witnessed her over-medicated state when they had first arrived at the house, then her tirade with her manager. Now here she was crying into his shoulder in the middle of the night.

Ehvah rolled her eyes and cringed. He must think she was a crazy person. Playing the damsel in distress was not her thing. For some reason he brought out the vulnerable side of her, almost like she was laid bare. No facades, no pretend, no celebrity. With David, she was who she was. She looked up to see her smiling face in the distant mirror. She liked that she didn't have to pretend with him.

Their conversations had revealed he was both wise and intelligent. His physical strength was obvious, but he had strength of character too. She knew she was attracted to him in a physical sense, but she was beginning to rely on him in an emotional sense as well.

Maybe I'm relying on him simply because he's here.

Perhaps her growing obsession was because she didn't have anyone else in her life right now. He was one solid, honest presence in an otherwise uncertain existence.

I'm going to have to get out more.

She lay wide awake for a few minutes, contemplating her capacity for socialization before a gentle knock at the doorway made her jump.

"Sorry, I didn't mean to startle you."

Ehvah had estimated David was well over six foot, but from her lower position on the bed he looked huge. His frame filled the doorway.

"I'm not asleep." She shifted up the bed.

"I wanted to let you know that I've dealt with Boof. He won't snooze on the job again."

"Thanks."

He turned to go, then swung back.

"I know a bit about nightmares. There was a period where I suffered with them myself. I can sleep on the sofa if you like." He motioned to the settee that took up one corner of the master bedroom. "Sometimes it makes a difference, knowing there's someone else in the room."

Ehvah opened her mouth to reject his offer, considering her recent revelation regarding her reliance on his presence, but then the memory of the peace she felt in his arms resurfaced. He was right. It would be comforting knowing he was there with her. Besides, making her feel safe was part of his job description.

"That would be great. Thanks. There's a spare pillow and a blanket in the cupboard."

He retrieved the linen and made himself as comfortable as a large man could on a modest settee.

Ehvah smiled at the sight of his legs hanging off the end of the furniture, but at the same time gratitude overcame her at his kind gesture.

She lay awake for some time, feeling his presence in the room with her. For a second she wondered what it would be like to have his body next to hers. That thought send tingles up her spine.

What would he do if she went over to him? Her mind raced through dangerous scenarios. She imagined moist, hot lips covering hers. Heat and sweat engulfing their colliding bodies.

This may be worse than the nightmare.

A loud snort shattered her fantasy.

Humph. Even his snoring's attractive.

She listened to his heavy breathing for a few moments before she fell into a dreamless sleep.

CHAPTER 13

Ehvah took a deep breath, filling her lungs with salty air. There was an intense rawness in being this close to the sea. The wind was wild today, and the pounding of the waves produced a hypnotic rhythm that lulled her into a delightful calm. The red-winged cockatoos were still in the area. She could hear their squawking in the distance as they devoured coastal berries. They made her smile.

Ehvah looked out towards the white wash of the ocean. Every aspect of this place had done her good. The environment, the isolation, and the company.

She was seeing a psychologist who 'got' her, and she had discovered that a good professional's job was to guide her to finding her own answers, not telling her what to think and do.

Her sessions with Ron Murray had brought her to two conclusions. The first was that she had suffered some kind of breakdown when she had stopped working. Her identity had been wrapped up in her work, an easy crutch to fall on after every person she had loved had died. Now she had to forge a new life. This time, it had to be a life linked to who she was, not who the world wanted her to be.

She had reached a second conclusion after last night's terror. It was time to do something about James's death. She didn't know what, but she had to fix things.

But how, God? I wish a solution could drop in my lap. I know I haven't spoken much to you since Gran died, but I know you're up there. I need your help.

David appeared at the entrance to the track that lead to the beach. He hadn't been in her room when she had woken that morning, now as he strained to climb each step she saw the effects of cramping his body onto the settee.

Boof walked out to meet his colleague, a packed sub sandwich in his hand.

"Hey, man, did you have any beach to run on? There's a big tide today. Looks like it's right up to the top of the bank." His voice was muffled by a mouthful of food.

"You do know this is not your house, right?" David moved into a stretch while looking at his partner.

Boof stopped mid-chew to give David a bemused glance, then motioned over to her.

"Ehvah said I could make a snack".

She had to smile. Boof's idea of a snack was more than what most people ate for an entire meal.

"Don't worry," he said. "I made her one too."

Ehvah picked up the plate next to her that held the stacked sandwich. As much as her appetite had improved, she did not find this particular delicacy appetizing. She had taken a few bites to be polite, but hadn't been able to get any further.

"How can you eat that for breakfast?" David shook his head at Boof.

"What?" Boof's mouth was full again. "It's a bacon and egg sanga. With a few extras." He pointed to the sandwich layers. "Fried pineapple, baked beans, cheese. It's good. You want one?"

Ehvah laughed. Boof had the stature of a giant and the innocence of a child. It was easy to forgive his slip-up during the night.

"No, thank you. I'll let you both enjoy your breakfast while I have a shower." David peeled off his singlet, saturated with sweat.

Ehvah had a flashback to last night's mental vision of their colliding bodies, and the sweat it would generate.

Don't look at him.

Memories of how safe she had felt being held by him popped into her mind, and a burning heat crept up her neck.

Stop thinking about him.

But it was too late. She couldn't help but stare as he

moved towards the door.

Wow. He's ripped.

Ugh. You idiot. You need to get out more.

"How are you feeling?" He paused at the door and looked over at her.

Ehvah felt like a deer in headlights. She averted her gaze to the sandwich. Had he noticed her staring? Burning heat flooded her body from head to toe.

"Uh, not too bad. No more nightmares, so that's good." She glanced up to see if he was satisfied with her answer, but all she got back was a dark stare.

Of course he knows you were checking him out.

If there was one thing Ehvah had realized about her security man, it was that he didn't miss a thing. She had never seen anyone as aware of their environment as David. At times it was unnerving. No doubt he had seen her Google attempt too.

She half expected him to tease her over her voyeurism, but he gave her a tight-lipped smile. His look could be interpreted as smugness over her all too obvious crush. Her embarrassment morphed into an artificial irritation.

You really think you're something, don't you?

That was unfair. She had spent enough time around David to know that he wasn't egotistical, but in that moment it was a lot safer to peg him as proud rather than deathly attractive.

His smile finally reached his eyes, and her negativity crumbled under his warmth.

"That's good to hear."

"Hey, you still right for tonight?" Boof cut in on their exchange.

David turned to his friend. "Oh, yeah." He covered the few meters to the end of her seat. "I forgot to tell you."

Ehvah scrambled to sit up.

"There's a change in schedule. I've got to go out tonight, so Boof will be here from five p.m. to six a.m. instead of coming in late."

"Where are you going?"

The words were out of her mouth before Ehvah had a

chance to think.

Not cool.

"Well, I've committed to something." He rubbed the back of his neck.

"Do you have a hot date?"

That is so not your business.

"I have a date of sorts. I wouldn't call it hot. I won't be far away. I just need to skip over to the next beach." He frowned and focused on his feet.

Boof snickered in the background. "It's a hot date alright. At least, it's been hot before." He followed his vague statement with a deep rolling chuckle.

David shook his head at Boof, before turning back to her. "Trust me, it's nothing interesting, just a favor for a friend."

"If it's not a big deal, I'll just come with you." Somewhere in the back of her mind an alarm bell went off, but she ignored it, adding, "I need an outing."

His eyebrows rose. "That's impossible. I can't look after you there. You'll have to stay here with Boof. Besides, you're not supposed to leave the house without prior approval."

"Excuse me?" Ehvah reeled back in confusion. What was he talking about? "What approval?"

David sighed and slapped his shirt over his shoulders. "I don't know, but the boss told me we had to log any of your outings with him prior to execution."

His bemused look and mediocre explanation didn't satisfy her. All attractiveness of his bare torso evaporated and Ehvah felt a tide of fury and confusion rush in.

What on earth is going on?

She scooted to the end of the daybed and stood to face him, knocking over the sandwich in the process.

"So what are you saying? Am I some sort of prisoner here?"

"That's a bit dramatic." He held up a hand in her direction. "You're no prisoner. I'm not making any rules. I'm just following the brief."

"Well, who dictated this brief?" Ehvah placed her hands on her hips and stared him down.

"I don't know who. I only know what the boss told me." David had both hands up now. He dropped his hands and looked over to Boof. The big man was munching away, casually watching them like he was sitting in a cinema.

"It was your aunt." Boof swallowed before continuing. "She said we had to check in with her before you went anywhere. She made us sign a confident paper."

"You mean a confidentiality agreement." David frowned.

Boof pointed at him.

"Yeah, that thing. We were pretty confident we could do the job, though. I don't know why she thought we needed some paper. She rings the boss every coupla days. He can't stand her. Sometimes he makes me talk to her, but she's real hard to understand. She usually hangs up on me." He flashed a lopsided grin.

Ehvah couldn't believe it. Her aunt's so-called protection was nothing more than a way of keeping her under control. Over the last few weeks it had been easy to forget Mara. Even though she was a short distance away, the house felt like her little bubble of paradise. And she had thought she was rid of Mara's spying when she left the hotel.

Ehvah had reveled in the fact that her aunt was otherwise occupied and leaving her alone. It looked as though Mara was much closer than she had thought. It would also explain why she hadn't received one phone call from Mara the entire time she'd been here. Her aunt knew all about her daily routine. All this time she'd been enjoying the peace, yet these guys had been spying on her for her aunt. So much for them being her friends.

A burning sense of betrayal bit at her insides. How dare they all treat her like a child. She could feel her jaw stiffen.

"Let's get one thing straight. From now on I'm the boss. I go where I like, when I like. With or without you. Do you both understand?" Her voice was so loud it echoed off the mountains.

David's expression was unreadable. His eyes gave nothing away. It was Boof who spoke.

"Sure thing, boss."

His happy tone was in such opposition to the situation, it

fired her temper.

"I'm the one paying your wages, not my aunt. She doesn't have any money. Don't forget it."

With that she walked through the door, slamming it behind her.

CHAPTER 14

Mara checked the caller ID on her cell before addressing the nearest crew member.

"It's my niece. I have to take it." She hit the connection button.

"Who do you think you are?" Ehvah didn't bother with pleasant greetings before launching into attack mode.

Mara took a breath and steeled for a showdown.

"What are you taking about?"

"As if you don't know. Telling the security company to report my every move to you is plain crazy. Maybe you're as loony as your mother."

Mara felt a surge of heat flow through her body. She moved away from the set and into a private area

"My mother was a star. A bigger one than you'll ever be."

"Your mother was in and out of mental institutions, and in between those stints she got married and divorced. Notice a genetic pattern?"

Mara could feel the pressure on her fingers as they gripped the cell, and the tendons in her neck begin to throb.

I hate her. Hate her.

"I may have a few ex-husbands floating around, but you're the one seeing the shrink, Ehvah."

"Because your latest ex-husband was a criminal. And now you think you can control my life?"

Mara balled her free hand into a fist. She tightened and released it in an attempt to gain some control. She took a deep breath and forced composure before replying.

"I told the security company that you've been distraught,

and to watch you closely as you were suffering from shock," she said in an even tone. "That's the reason I asked them to report back to me."

There was a pause at the end of the line.

Mara could feel her chest heaving under the period corset she was wearing. If Ehvah didn't buy her excuse, she didn't know what she would do.

"Do you know anything about the pills?"

Her heart skipped a beat. "What pills?" She pounded the toe of one boot into the dirt.

"The sleeping pills I was taking. They were wrong. Who did you send to pack up my stuff at the hotel?"

"A staff member from the shoot. Why?" She hoped her voice sounded suitably perplexed.

"I think someone switched my tablets from sleeping pills to some sort of tranquilizer."

"Well, I don't know anything about that. Why would anyone from here switch your tablets? Maybe they built up in your system and you had a bad reaction to them."

She didn't reply.

"Ehvah, I've done everything I can to help you. Accusing me of being some sort of control freak is not helping the situation. Are you staying in the house for a little longer?" Mara kicked the ground harder, sending plumes of dust onto the hem of her skirt.

"I have to go home sometime, but I haven't made up my mind when."

Good. We need more time.

"I'm here for at least another week, so the place is all yours," Mara said.

"Fine. I've told the security company that I'm in charge, so don't expect any more reports from them. After all, it's my money that's paying them."

The throbbing ache in her forehead flared. Of course it was her money. It was always her money. But not for long.

"How could I forget?"

Hanging up the call, she established a connection with Lyle's cell.

He answered in one ring.

"Forget what I said about your family. Do whatever it takes to get into that house."

***

David breathed a sigh of relief as he stepped out of the car. The afternoon had been a nightmare.

A shopping trip was a standard activity, but Ehvah had done her best to stretch the limits of his professionalism. She had skipped from one shop to the next, ducking and weaving between racks of clothing and jumping in and out of dressing rooms in an obvious effort to make his job difficult.

The one reprieve he had had was when she had been fixed to the hairdresser's chair for two hours.

David knew what she was trying to do. This was all about asserting her authority. He didn't blame her. He viewed the situation with her aunt as entirely unfair. Ehvah was a grown woman. She had the right to do as she pleased, and she had a right to be angry.

His boss had filled him in that morning. Mara's focus was keeping her niece contained. Not once had she inquired after her wellbeing. The pair had a strained relationship at best, and revealing that Mara knew all about Ehvah's daily routine had hit a sensitive nerve in his charge.

Even with the dragon relative breathing down Ehvah's neck, right now he was having a hard time feeling sorry for her. Not when she had spent the day taking out her frustrations on him.

"You can put those packages in my room."

She pointed to the back of the sporty car they had rented. David looked up from the trunk to see her walk to the entrance of the house.

"I would prefer it if you let me go into the house before you," he called to her retreating back.

She turned and gave him a death stare. Her much shorter groomed hair swung around the top of her shoulders as she moved. If she hadn't been so committed to putting him in his place, he would have complimented her on the new style. It suited her. The subtle tones of blonde and light brown made her green eyes more vibrant, even if golden flecks flashed angry vibes his way.

Twice during the outing, he had caught himself watching her so intently that he had forgotten to scan the area. He found himself drifting into the memory of holding her last night, something he still couldn't believe he'd done. It was unprofessional and out of character, but at the same time, it had seemed the right and natural thing to do. The tension between them worried him. He didn't need any distractions, especially not in the form of a client—and she was distracting him beyond any limit he had ever known.

Right now those big green eyes bore laser beams of displeasure at him.

"That's not necessary. Just do as I ask." She swung her bag over her shoulder and strutted to the door as fast as she could in tight jeans and high heels.

David watched her walk away, noticing the sway of her hips. Her frame had filled out in the last few weeks and curves contoured her body. A stirring of desire crept in, followed by an instant application of forced control. He gritted his teeth.

"Lord, help me get over this quick." He picked up the shopping, closed the trunk and moved inside to dump the bags in her bedroom. He stepped out onto the veranda in the hope that some fresh sea air would soothe him. Unfortunately she had beaten him to the location. She lolled on one of the chairs, writing in her journal.

"Get me a can of soda?" She didn't look up as she repositioned her legs.

The command was so obnoxious that David's patience snapped.

"Get it yourself."

"Excuse me?"

"I said, get it yourself. Waiting on you is not part of my job description."

Ehvah put the book down on the side table and glared at him.

"Oh, so has my aunt dictated your job description as well?"

David shook his head. "Man, when you get your back

up, watch out."

The heavy set of her jaw spoke volumes.

"I thought you were here for me. That we had become friends, but all the while you're spying on me for my aunt."

"I'm just trying to do my job. I wasn't aware of the situation with your aunt until Boof filled us both in. I've never met or spoken to your aunt, but considering the state you were in when we first arrived, logging your movements seemed like a plausible request. After that was sorted and you improved, I didn't give the directive a second thought until this morning."

She stood up and placed her hands on her hips.

"Do you really expect me to believe that?"

"My job is making sure you're safe. I had a brief. I was executing it."

"Great, so now I'm not a person, I'm a brief. Maybe you should go back to the army, because its obvious people are just assignments to you."

She shifted her weight from one foot to the next, hands still on hips. He recalled what those swaying hips had done to him minutes ago. Looking at her face didn't help, because then an overwhelming urge to kiss her hit him with full force. It was so strong that it forced him into stunned silence.

Get a grip. Seriously.

His internal pep talk failed. He still wanted to kiss her, and now he was worried that whatever he did or said would lead to that happening. "I think we both need to cool down and reassess this situation."

Her brow furrowed low and her lips thinned out into a sharp line. He could see the red flush of anger seep up from her neck onto her cheeks to cover her forehead.

"Don't patronize me like I'm some lower being. I'm a star. Who are you? You're just a security guard. What have you done in your life?"

For a second David couldn't believe the insult. Then all the stress of the day combined with a sense of panic at his reaction to her forced something inside him to snap.

"Don't go making assumptions about my life when you've spent yours cocooned in a bubble of privilege."

Her mouth fell open and eyes widened.

"How dare you!"

There was something about her stance. The way she stomped the floor, the balled fists and locked jaw all reminded him of a two–year-old in the throes of a temper tantrum.

"You know what you are?"

"As if you would know!"

"A spoiled brat." He crossed his arms and set his stance.

Her lips pursed and cheeks fumed red. "How dare you. Get out."

She extended one arm, her finger pointing to the door, the other still firm on her hip.

David felt his anger subside, and a horrible realization take its place. Did he just insult a client?

What on earth are you doing? You're out of control.

He closed his eyes for a second and tried to tap into sanity. What was happening to him? His mind skimmed over the range of difficult clients he had endured over the years. Some of them had treated him far worse than Ehvah had that day. Why had this affected him?

Too much time.

They were holed up here together, day in and day out. It stood to reason that eventually that would become a problem. She was right, he had to get out. He looked at his watch.

"Boof'll be here any minute. I'll organize for someone else to take my place on this job."

He took a few steps towards the door before turning back. She had crossed her arms and was looking out to the ocean.

"I apologize for my comment. I don't know what your life has been like. I am your friend. I wasn't fully aware of the situation with your aunt until this morning, and I'm sorry I said you were a brat—even if it has been true today."

He couldn't help adding the last rebuke before going to the servant's quarters to pack.

CHAPTER 15

Ehvah looked over at Boof as he maneuvered the car around a narrow turn. They travelled through thick rainforest foliage that created a canopy over the last stretch of Millionaire's Row.

It had been easy to convince him to drive her to see David. After Boof's initial reluctance, Ehvah had lured him into her plan by telling him he could drive the sports car. "Besides," she had said to him, "It will be nice to get out for a change, and I'll go on my own if you don't take me. I am the boss—remember?"

She didn't tell Boof about her ulterior motive. She had an apology to deliver.

It was bad enough that David had called her a spoiled brat, but when she thought back on her actions during the day, she realized she had acted like one. She had been angry about having been treated like a child, then she had behaved like one, taking her frustrations out on him.

He had become her friend, and she hadn't had a true friendship in a long time. She had blown it. A mass of sorrys circulated her head as they drew closer to the venue one beach south of Millionaire's Row.

Maybe I can convince him to come back?

A sick pain in her stomach swirled at the thought of David not accepting her apology.

"This thing's ballistic."

Boof played with the button that opened the convertible soft top. Ehvah could see him grinning through the dull interior lights.

"Is it easy to handle, Boof?"

He tapped on the steering wheel in time with the radio music.

"Yeah, she's a beauty."

"Do we have much further to go?"

"Just up here." He glanced over to her. "You sure you wanna go to this thing?"

"How bad can it be?" Ehvah shrugged her shoulders. Boof had told her David was at a dance.

"I dunno." He backed off the accelerator as they entered a built-up area. "Doesn't seem like your sort of scene."

"Why?"

Ehvah had thought that she would fit right in at a dance. She picked up the choreography for her music videos and concerts, and although she wasn't a trained dancer, she could hold her own on the floor. Performance was in her blood.

Boof pulled into a narrow street. "You'll see what I mean."

Ehvah frowned at his cryptic reply.

As they reached the end of the road, it was clear where the party was. Cars were parked off the road at all angles, as well as being scattered across a grassed area leading up to a long narrow building.

"What does C.W.A. stand for?" she asked. The letters were lit up over the top of a timber arch above the door. Two floodlights illuminated the outside.

Boof found a piece of grass to park on.

"Um, Country Women's Association, I think. My mum's in it." He killed the engine.

A vibrant beat came from the hall. The tune was revealed when Ehvah opened her door. It was an old rock-and-roll song.

Boof met her at the back of the car.

"Now, if they get a bit handsy, you just let me know and I'll sort them out. The ladies are all over me, so the men are probably gonna be worse with you."

"What?"

Women all over him? What sort of event is this?

"Don't worry, I'll look after you."

He gestured to the short staircase leading to the open door.

She shrugged. It couldn't be any rougher than the L.A. club scene. After all, the band was playing *Johnny B. Goode*. She paused in the doorway to take in the event.

The large hall was full of elderly men and women, each one dancing up a storm. Some were jiving, others were swaying to the music. There was one couple doing a lively quickstep. Some of the women danced together, while several groups danced in circles.

The band was located on a small platform at the back of the hall. Ehvah recognized the bass player—it was her psychologist, Dr. Murray. She had picked him to be in his late forties, but in a fifties rock-and-roll costume and surrounded by retirees, he looked a lot younger.

As the song came to the famous guitar solo, a channel parted between the dancers, providing Ehvah with a view of the entire band.

"Oh, my goodness." She grabbed Boof's arm in shock as David stepped forward and completed the solo. His fingers moved with skill up and down the arm of the electric guitar.

She turned to see Boof jiggling his upper body moving in tune with the music.

"I didn't know he played," she yelled over the noise.

"Yeah, he's good, hey?"

Solo completed, David stepped back.

He's amazing. She couldn't believe it.

"Excuse me, young lady." An elderly gentleman dressed in a patterned shirt and long trousers stood before her, his hand outstretched. "Would you care to dance?"

"I would love to." She placed her hand in his.

"Hey," Boof yelled. "No wandering hands, old man." He waved a finger in mock authority.

The elderly gentleman poked his tongue back at Boof.

Ehvah covered her mouth in shock, and attempted to stifle a laugh as she was pulled onto the dance floor.

She wasn't familiar with the jive, but thought maybe that was the closest dance to whatever they were doing. It was so much fun to be twisted and twirled, and during one vibrant maneuver, she was grateful for the fact that she had worn a pair of white jeans and not a skirt. Her shirt was fitted, but had floating lace sleeves. They flounced around her, as did her new hairstyle that floated around her face.

After two rock-and-roll songs, the band began a slow organ-based melody, and the gentleman pulled her into a waltz.

They had moved a few steps when a large form appeared behind him, tapping his shoulder.

"Mind if I cut in?" David's formidable bulk towered over them.

"Thank you, young lady. It was a great pleasure." The man dropped his stance and stepped aside with a bow.

"For me too." Ehvah gave him her best smile.

David swung her into a dancing pose, one hand splayed her lower back and the other held hers captive. She had no choice but to move with him.

They traveled a few steps before he spoke.

"What are you doing here?" He pulled back to stare at her. His brown eyes looked even deeper against the chocolate color of his polo shirt.

Ehvah felt a nervous flutter in her stomach, which was made worse by the awareness of his touch.

"I . . . uh. I just wanted a chance to—"

"Where's Boof?"

"I left him at the door." She looked around to get her bearings.

"So he's here with you?"

"Yeah. How do you think I got here?" She could feel her defensiveness rise at the sharpness in his tone.

David tilted his head towards the stage. "Don't worry, I see him."

Boof was on the raised platform doing a spectacular air guitar performance in sync with the organist's waltz.

The sight was so comical that Ehvah burst into giggles.

She looked up to see David with a broad smile on his face as well.

"He's a bit different, isn't he?"

At that moment, Boof flung his hand aloft in a passionate salute to rock, his massive bulk shuddering with the movement.

She giggled harder while David shook his head. They spent a moment avoiding a collision with another couple before Ehvah spoke.

"I didn't know you played guitar."

David gave a shrug.

"My mother taught piano. She persevered with me for years before she gave up and allowed me to learn the guitar instead."

"You're really good. Have you ever played professionally?"

"For a few years. It's the old story: young band, big dreams, even bigger egos, no money. That kind of thing. I eventually gave it up and joined the army."

Ehvah took a moment to acknowledge her ex-dancing partner as he twirled past her with a new lady.

"That's a pretty big change. Aspiring rock star to soldier."

David's hand left her waist as they reached the edge of the crowd.

"Not really. Remember—I have a long heritage of military service."

Ehvah felt a sense of loss as he released her hand.

"Come on, I'll get you a drink."

She followed him to a long table set up on the side of the hall. Two elderly ladies in fifties costumes were serving refreshments.

One asked her if she would sign a napkin for her granddaughter. Ehvah obliged with pleasure. It was a delightful feeling to be recognized with such grace.

She accepted a plastic cup of punch from the other lady and walked with David to a side door leading onto a veranda.

There were a few others out there, enjoying the freshness of the evening. She had been told May was a good month to visit the Australian tropics. The days were still warm, and at times, humid, but the evenings were fresh and cool. A clear sky held a multitude of stars that lit up the night.

The area was semi-rural with the occasional house scattered through sugarcane fields. Ehvah could make out a barrier of cane at the back of the building. Tall, thin stalks clumped together with green, grassy tops, and a grass spear jutted out from each tall stick. In one of their previous conversations, David had explained that the industry was in the cutting and processing season. The colorful spears were an indication that the field was ready to harvest. The air was tinged with the plant's sweet, grassy scent.

She wondered how far this field stretched back. Sugarcane fields seemed to pop up all over the district.

They moved to the far end of the veranda, away from the entry point and adjacent to the doorway leading to the stage. It was darker there, and the stars looked even more brilliant now they were away from the main doors and the light spilling out of the hall.

They stood for a second before Ron Murray appeared at the side door.

"Hey, Dave, ten minutes and we'll kick off again. That alright with you?" He called down to them.

"No worries." David saluted with his plastic cup.

"Hey there, Ehvah. It's great to see you out and about. I hope you've got your dancing shoes on. I just overheard an argument about who gets to partner you next." The doctor winked.

"Ready and willing, Doctor Murray," she called back.

"Please, call me Ron. I'm Rock-and-Roll Ron tonight." He chuckled at his self-proclaimed moniker.

"I'll see you in there."

He then disappeared back through the door.

"Who knew Dr. Murray was all about the music." Ehvah put a hand on the weathered timber rail.

David backed up against the adjoining angle.

"It used to drive me crazy when he wanted me to fill in at these events, but I'm beginning to enjoy them. At least it's a little cooler now. The last one they held was in the middle of January, and it was stinking hot. We had one lady admitted to hospital for dehydration."

"Oh, so that's what Boof meant by a hot date."

A minute of uncomfortable silence fell between them before he spoke.

"So, what's this all about? I can't imagine you came here for the entertainment." He peered over the rim of his cup.

Nervous tension formed a prickly feeling at the back of her neck.

"Well . . ." She stalled, sipping her drink.

"Hmm?" David's mouth lifted at the corners.

Ehvah looked into her cup. A piece of pineapple was bobbing in the liquid.

Just say it.

She wasn't accustomed to delivering dramatic apologies, and all the stalling was making it much worse.

Spit it out.

Willing herself to do it wasn't helping either.

She took a deep breath.

"I didn't want you to leave without telling you that I'm sorry. I was angry, and I took it out on you. That wasn't fair." Her stomach lurched. She couldn't look at him, so she concentrated on the bobbing fruit.

"I deserved to be told off. I treated you badly, and I am sorry. It's just that . . . I haven't had a good friend like you in a long time. Maybe ever. I don't want to lose you. I mean, you know, your friendship and everything . . ." She cringed, just listening to herself.

Shut up.

She willed her mouth to stop and peeked up at him.

His head was tilted to one side and for once his eyes held their old warmth.

"Apology accepted."

She smiled with relief. Maybe he didn't think she was a complete moron.

"Does that mean you'll come back to work? Because I don't want some random person I don't know there. I want you to stay."

She had been in a semi-panic all day. He had become such a stable presence in her life. Being here without him was unthinkable.

Now it was David's turn to glare into his cup.

"Do you have fruit in your drink?" A frown furrowed his brow.

"What?"

"Fruit. In your drink?"

Ehvah swirled her cup. "I've got a piece of pineapple. Why?"

"I've got a grape, and something that looks like a cashew nut."

"Really?"

David looked straight at her. His deep brown eyes gleamed in the soft light. "Look." He held out his cup.

She peered into the rim and burst out in a fit of giggles.

"That does look like a cashew nut."

They both laughed as he fished it out and hurtled the offensive floater into the cane paddock.

A scraping noise from inside the hall made them both turn to the door. Boof was on the stage and had taken a seat at the drum kit. His body jiggled as he tapped the sticks to the cymbal. A faint ting graduated into a clang.

"What is he doing?" David shook his head. His forehead creased.

Ehvah smiled at the sight of Boof trying to form a beat succession. The disjointed bashing was a complete failure.

She indicated the big man inside and turned to David.

"Are you seriously going to leave me to Boof?"

He turned back to her. She felt the shallow breath in her chest as his eyes held hers.

"So will you come back?"

Ehvah could see his shoulders rise and fall in sync with the rhythm of his breathing. During Boof's distraction their bodies had swayed closer so that Ehvah could feel the warmth radiating from him. A great part of her wanted him closer. She sensed her body sway into him.

He was so close that she could reach up and touch his face. She thought about doing it for a second, but steadied her hand by her side. He blinked as his gaze held hers.

"I like your haircut. You look beautiful."

He reached up and ran a strand of hair through his

fingers.

His compliment made her stomach flutter and her already racing heart felt like it was running a marathon. The hand by her side lifted, but instead of touching his face, it settled on his chest. Ehvah could feel his thunderous heartbeat under her hand.

Her lips parted as he moved to grip her waist. Ehvah tilted her head up as he pulled her to him.

Their lips were almost touching when a massive crash reverberated through the hall.

She froze as they both looked towards the doorway. The drum kit stands had collapsed, and Boof was flat on his back under the stage.

CHAPTER 16

"It's not serious."

David pulled on his seatbelt, then shuffled into a more comfortable position behind the steering wheel.

"He'll have to stay in bed for a few days, but Boof'll love that." He started the engine and glanced behind to reverse the sports car out of its spot.

"It's lucky the instruments weren't damaged."

David looked back to see Ehvah fastening her belt.

"That seat wasn't meant to hold the likes of Boof." He found first gear. The drum stool had collapsed, and Boof had fallen off the platform, landing in an awkward position.

"I hope he recovers soon."

Ehvah fiddled with the switches in the center console of the car.

David tried to ignore the tension between them as they drove along the coastline. The silence was palpable.

He'd had one significant relationship in between army deployments. It had ended over a year ago, and he had been single since. He wasn't immune to the opposite sex, but lately he wondered if he had become immune to relationships. His nomadic lifestyle suited him. Taking on a partner felt like more of a chore than a blessing. But that was before this job. And this girl.

The risk is too high.

The thought pulled him up. His training had taught him to weigh up risks. Could he apply this strategy to his life too?

He glanced across at Ehvah. Her blonde hair framed her face in soft waves and the night light flooding the cabin danced shadows over her features. He thought about how his pulse raced at seeing her there tonight, especially after having decided to walk away and never see her again. For his own sanity.

David felt a stirring in his gut far more potent than desire. He was falling for this woman, and that made working for her too great a risk.

Why now, Lord? Why this woman? It can't work.

Something deep inside told him it could. David shook his head at his confusion, then glanced across at Ehvah to see if she had noticed. She was looking out her window.

It was a spectacular view. The risen moon cast a channel of yellow across the ocean. The navy mass of water twinkled with a million reflections of light. The diamond-topped waves and palm tree shadows flashed by as they entered the twisting range leading to Millionaire's Row.

"This country is amazing. I think I need to get out and see more of it." Ehvah shifted to face the front of the car.

David seizing on her desire for adventure.

"Maybe that's what you should do. Go down south and check out the southern states. Sydney and Melbourne. There's a lot to cover down there. Or over to the Territory and visit Uluru. It's a mind-blowing experience, standing at the base of that big rock."

He paused to negotiate a turn.

"The west has some must-do's, like feeding the wild dolphins at Monkey Mia, or flying over the Bungle Bungles—that's another natural rock formation."

Ehvah had sat up a little straighter during his 'go see Australia' speech. She was interested.

"That sounds amazing. Will you come with me?"

Oh no. That was not what he expected.

"Don't you have some friends who'd like to travel with you? I'm sure you would know people who would like to see the country with you."

Her shoulders slumped.

"I was too busy to make close friends when I was working. My acquaintances were all work colleagues. When my contract ended, they all drifted off to new jobs. We never kept in touch. My recent friends were party people. I was happy to leave them behind."

She wriggled a little in her seat. "Besides, I'd still need security if I was travelling so it'll be a job, right?"

David took a deep breath. He knew he had to quit before this relationship morphed into something he had no control over, but throughout the afternoon his spirits had plummeted at the thought of not seeing her again. Then, as she was in his arms on the dance floor, he realized he had experienced a pang of jealousy over seeing her dance with the old man. It was ludicrous. He was in too deep, and if he hung around any longer, he was going to drown.

The best outcome was to go their separate ways.

"I can't do that, Ehvah." He gripped the wheel as he negotiated another tight bend.

"I don't know what's going on between us, but it's going nowhere. Maybe it was inevitable that two people who spend so much time in isolation were going to gravitate towards each other. But I don't get involved with my clients, and I don't do casual relationships. At the moment I don't do long-term ones either. You must see how crazy it is."

David slowed down on the narrow road that separated their section of coastline from the rest of the mainland. Out of the corner of his eye he could see Ehvah twisting her fingers in her lap.

"Well . . ." She broke off for a second. "We could just forget about what almost happened tonight and concentrate on being friends, couldn't we?"

David considered her suggestion, making a firm decision. "I can't see that happening."

"Why not?"

He pulled into the street leading to the house.

"Because I'm not sure it could be kept at that level. Not after tonight."

"You've got to be kidding." Her voice was high. "You think you're so attractive that I wouldn't be able to resist you?"

David pulled into the garage and turned the key before pivoting in his seat to face her.

"You know that's not what I think. I just feel that it's best we go our separate ways. Professionally and socially." He hoped his unwavering focus drove home his statement.

Ehvah blinked a few times then looked down. "Well, I guess that's it then."

David reached for the door handle.

Ehvah retrieved the house keys. She entered first. It was dark and silent.

David flipped the light switch but didn't follow her down the hall, choosing instead to throw his bag in his room. He had at least one more night here, thanks to Boof's injury. He had a feeling it was going to be a sleepless one.

He moved to close his door when a loud scream bellowed down the hallway, followed by the sound of breaking glass. A surge of adrenaline hit him full force as he sprang into action. The echo suggested the scream had come from the kitchen.

The room was dark, but as he entered he could make out a large form encompassing a smaller frame. They were moving in the direction of the veranda door. The smaller figure was kicking, and muffled sounds could be heard under what he knew to be a hand muzzle.

He bolted forward and used his weight to knock all three of them to the floor. The force of the fall separated the two figures and David addressed the larger, knowing the smaller one to be Ehvah.

He didn't wait for the rising attacker to gain any bearing. Using his fighting skills, he put the intruder back on the ground. To his surprise, the man recovered in an instant and wasted no time retaliating. They traded blows, knocking over a side table as they fought for the upper hand.

It occurred to David that this was someone who knew how to fight. He was just about to charge the man again when the light came on. The bright flash blinded him for a second before he focused on the man's face.

Another surge of adrenaline hit him, followed by numb realization as recognition set in.

Both he and his sparring partner stopped dead in their tracks.

David was about to address him when a large object

bore down on his opponent's head. A heavy clunk sounded, followed by a thud as the man dropped to the ground.

Ehvah stood behind his crumpled body, holding a heavy brass vase.

CHAPTER 17

"Call nine-one-one."

Ehvah could feel her heart racing with the speed of a rocket.

The intruder was on all fours, groaning and holding his head. A visible wound oozed blood onto the carpet. He looked up and cursed.

Ehvah jumped back. She could feel her whole body shake as he unleashed a torrent of violent, insulting words. Her indignation rose at a particularly nasty phrase, and her shaking intensified in the presence of her anger.

How dare you?

Without thinking she kicked out a leg out and connected with his ribcage. The aggressive maneuver hurt her foot. It hurt him too, because he screamed several new curse words while clutching his side.

"Ehvah, it's okay." David grabbed her in a bear hug and pulled her away.

"What?"

"I know this guy. It's okay. He's good."

She felt her face contort.

"Get that chick away from me." The man's voice was strong considering he had just suffered two serious blows.

One glance at him riled her again. "How dare you. You . . ."

Driven by renewed anger, she reached for him with her other foot. It was a futile effort, because David had her in a strong hold.

"Ehvah, chill out."

It started to register what he had said. "You know this

guy?"

"Yes."

"Who is he?"

"If you settle down, I'll tell you."

David's voice was cool and calm. The opposite of how she felt.

Ehvah took several deep breaths, and allowed her body to relax a little. She had a moment's realization that she was back in his arms, when David released her.

"Are you going to be cool?"

She could still feel her heart beating fast, and her hands started to shake, but she nodded in an effort to reassure him she would be still. He remained close, looking down at her. One of his eyes was puffy and pink.

"You're safe, okay?" He reached out one hand to rest on her shoulder.

Maybe it was the gesture, or the way his eyes searched hers, but a wave of heat swept through her and her eyes filled with tears. She looked down at the man on the floor, who was still trying to catch his breath.

He attacked me.

Ehvah swallowed hard in an attempt to hold back the shock. David moved his hand from her shoulder to cradle the side of her face. His other hand followed so that he held her face in his hands. His chocolate brown eyes were so warm and caring that Ehvah felt a tear squeeze out the side of one eye. It travelled down her cheek where he wiped it away with a thumb.

Seconds later, he had to do the same for the other cheek.

"Are you sure you need security? You're definitely a fighter." He winked, and she smiled in response. He pulled her to him and placed a warm kiss on her forehead. For a second everything else was forgotten.

"Hey, mate, if you have a moment, I could do with some first aid." The intruder had pulled himself onto the couch. He had removed his t-shirt and was holding it against a wound that ran with blood.

He was a big man. Not as tall as David, but just as

muscular. Tattoos covered both his arms, and were also visible on his torso. His hair was cropped short against his skull. He looked like someone not to be messed with.

David went over to check his wound, while Ehvah gave her attacker what she hoped was an evil eyed look.

"She got you a beauty." David screwed his face up at the cut.

The man gave a scowl.

"Ehvah, could you get me a bowl with some water, and a towel? There's a first aid kit under the sink." David looked over to her.

Ehvah moved to the kitchen to fulfil the request, while still listening to their conversation.

"This is not how I thought I'd be catching up with you," the man said. "I flew in this morning and went over to the boat. They told me you were on a job."

David grinned.

I don't see what's so funny.

"This is my job." David said. "What are you doing here?"

"This is my job, too."

David reached down from his elevated position and slapped his shoulder. "Well, mate, it doesn't seem to be working out for you."

Ehvah spotted the same currawong tattoo as David's on the man's shoulder as she moved back into the lounge. She placed the bowl of water on the coffee table adjacent to where the man was sitting.

"Yeah? Well, it looks like it's working out for you." The man's voice had a teasing tone. "I might have to make a career move into security. Looks like that's where the action is."

David maintained his smile as Ehvah passed him the towel. His jovial response to her attack was becoming exasperating.

What could be so amusing?

"Hold still. I'll see what I can do." David wet the towel and the man dropped his shirt. One corner was soaked with blood.

"So what sort of job are you on that has you doing

break-ins? I thought you'd given up the shady stuff."

The man drew a sharp breath as David held the towel to the side of his head.

"I did. Let's just say this called for a delicate touch. I owed someone a favor."

"Since when have you been delicate?"

"Since your girlfriend attacked me with a vase, man."

David laughed and rinsed the towel.

Ehvah crossed her arms. This was ridiculous. They were acting as though she wasn't there! And being called David's girlfriend heightened her infuriation. Especially as he had rejected her.

"Do you mind explaining how you two know each other, considering I was almost abducted a few minutes ago?"

David kept one hand on the wound. "Mark and I were in the same unit. We trained and served together."

"In the Marines?"

"In the SASR, love," Mark cut in.

Ehvah took a seat on the edge of the sofa opposite.

"So that's why you have the same tattoo? You're both Marines?"

"Army. Special operations," Mark said.

David placed the stained towel on the table.

"You need to share more, man." Mark indicated to Ehvah. "Chicks need to know stuff."

"Sure, because you're such an expert on women." David grabbed the first aid kit and pointed to Mark, while looking over at her. "Two wives."

"Three. Two ex, one wife-to-be."

"Three?" David broke out into a great laugh.

"Almost. That's what I wanted to see you about. Can you make it down for our engagement party?" Mark rubbed his side.

"I don't know. Depends on what your job here is about. If it involves her, it involves me."

Ehvah felt her insides do a cartwheel. Did he just claim loyalty to her? A bubble of hope surfaced.

Mark sat back against the cushion and looked between them.

"I guess I can't leave you in the dark. Handle what I say carefully."

"You know I will." David slapped a dressing over the wound.

Mark spread his legs out and pulled at his jeans. "You might want to sit down."

David took a place next to Ehvah.

"How much do you know about your uncle's business?" Mark looked at her.

"Nothing before he was murdered, but I know he was under investigation from the FBI. I don't know why. I can't remember him being in any trouble."

She turned to David. "James gave me regular updates, and everything was in order, as far as I knew. The FBI assured me my small portfolio wasn't a part of their investigation." She shrugged. "He was an all-round nice guy. To be honest, I always felt sorry for him being married to Mara. I still have a hard time believing he was doing anything illegal."

Mark raised his eyebrows. "Well, he was. He was laundering money for a Russian crime syndicate. He was skimming off the top, and they want their money back."

"No way." Ehvah felt her mouth drop.

"It's true." The intense glance Mark gave her confirmed his revelation.

"What does this have to do with why you're here?" David asked.

"Before he was killed, your uncle . . ." he pointed to Ehvah, " . . . transferred millions of the stolen money out of the account. The Russians don't know where he put it, but according to them, you . . ." he pointed to her again, " . . . know where it is."

Ehvah felt the blood rush out of her head and a numbness overcame her. She swallowed hard and jumped up in her seat.

"Why would they think I know where it is? I have no idea."

The two men looked back at her, expressionless.

"I have no idea. I swear." She could feel palpitations

pound her chest. "I can't believe this. I thought James was a great guy. He was always so good to me. Why would he do that?"

"It's okay. I believe you. We'll sort it out." David placed a hand on her leg.

She wiped her forehead. It felt sticky and wet. "Sort it out! I have Russian mobsters out for my blood." She fell back against the sofa and tried to control her shallow breathing.

"If it's any consolation, the Russians know you weren't involved in the scheme. Why would you steal money from them when you're already loaded?"

Mark pressed on the dressing as a trickle of blood broke through the fabric. "They assume your uncle planted the information on you because he knew they would have trouble getting to it."

"Are you sure about all this?" Ehvah whipped her head back up.

"What do you think I was doing here? I've been looking for the information. Would be handy to know what I'm looking for, but the Russians don't know. All I've been told is that you have the location of the money. Oh, and sorry about the mess in your room."

Ehvah felt her mouth drop open again. She hadn't been in her bedroom since they had returned. Who knew what state it was in after Mark had been there? She felt like getting up and giving him another kick in the ribs.

David was still. One finger rubbed at his bottom lip.

"You didn't expect us home?" he asked.

"No. I cased out the place for an hour, so I knew it was empty. When you came in you blocked my exit, so I jumped behind the counter and your girl ran right into me. I had to think on my feet."

A sick feeling bubbled in her gut. "Were you going to kill me?"

"Don't be stupid. I was going to get out the door and throw you back in. I didn't want you to see my face."

"But you work for the Russians."

"No. I don't even know any Russians. Well, apart from

my wife-to-be, but there's no connection."

David was smiling again. Ehvah couldn't take his flippant attitude. "Stop being so amused. This is not funny. This is my life. Your friend here is some sort of bad guy."

"Maybe in the past." He looked over at Mark. "Why did you agree to take this on?"

"A mate of mine was supposed to come, but he fell off his bike and broke something." Mark rolled his eyes.

David tilted his head and shrugged, questioning.

"I don't know the full story. He asked me to come instead. I shouldn't have, but it was the last favor I had owing and I figured why not get the slate completely clean."

David twisted his body to face her.

"Mark was in a biker gang. He recently decided to retire from the group."

"I won't leave altogether." Mark butted in. "They do some good work. Charity runs and stuff. I'm going to head that up."

"That's your call, mate. I think we should both be thankful that you did take this job. If you hadn't, we would've been in the dark, and whoever the Russians sent next might have actually known how to fight." David's cheeky grin revealed he was teasing his friend again.

Mark grunted. "Yeah, well, I wish them luck against this mad sheila."

Ehvah worked her face into her meanest pose. At least he didn't use a more colorful name this time. She knew 'sheila' was Aussie slang for woman. It was general rather than offensive.

She saw David stifle another grin.

"So where does the FBI fit into all this?" David asked.

"No idea. I only know what my mate told me. We're working for the Russian syndicate. He didn't mention any FBI." He reached over to grab his t-shirt. "I'd better get going."

Both men stood up and walked the few steps to the door. Ehvah made a start on tidying the coffee table. She saw Mark lean into David. He spoke quietly, but she still heard what he said.

"It's serious, mate. Best get her somewhere safe eh?"

A thumping noise followed, and she looked around to see them in a manly hug.

"Nice to see you with someone—finally." Mark said, still in a whisper. "Don't tell anyone she put me on the ground, will ya?"

"I'll keep it to myself." David replied.

"Good luck." Mark called over to her, then turned back to David. "Watch your back, bro."

David secured the lock and picked up the few things she couldn't carry.

"I'll take care of this stuff. Go and pack a bag. I'll take you to my place while we work out what to do."

Ehvah's spirits lifted. He was going to stay with her, and she needed his help now more than ever.

She managed to find a suitcase in the ransacked room and started packing.

It was impossible to get her head around everything that had happened. Why would James be involved in something like this? When did he plant this information on her? Where was it? And what did Mara have to do with it?

Ehvah closed her suitcase zipper as another thought played in her mind. What was she going to do about the snake tattoo?

CHAPTER 18

Visions of James's killer played on Ehvah's mind as she packed to leave. The eyewitness testimony she had hidden felt like a huge grey cloud hanging over her head. It wasn't fair to David to involve him any further when he didn't have all of the facts.

I have to tell him.

"All set?" David stood at her bedroom door.

As she had packed, Ehvah had mentally cataloged every one of her belongings in an attempt to rule out its significance to James and the information he had hidden on her. There was nothing she could tie to him.

"Yep."

She pulled her suitcase a few feet before David took over the task. They wasted no time packing the rental car and locking up the house.

Ehvah conceded mixed feelings as they drove away. She loved the beach house—it had been her sanctuary—but considering the night's events, she was relieved to be leaving for a safer location. She gave a heavy sigh as they exited Millionaire's Row.

"Are you okay?" David's concern echoed in her ears. Would he offer the same kindness when he discovered she had held back vital evidence?

"I'm a little shaken."

An overwhelming sense of gratitude at his presence overcame her. Hours earlier he had quit as her security man. Now he was prepared to stay and protect her. His promise was more than she deserved. Where would she be without him?

Thank you, God. Thank you.

Her heart ached with gratitude. Maybe there were times God did step in and save her day.

"It must be hard, considering all you've been through, but you have to trust that the Lord has a plan, even in this." David glanced over from driving before concentrating back on the road. "Faith always shows a way."

Ehvah thought again about the fact he was there with her.

"I have faith in you. I know you can protect me." Saying it aloud gave her a sense of hope.

David looked over at her, then braked. He pulled into a side street that ran adjacent to a beach.

"What are you doing?"

He parked the sports car before turning to her.

"Ehvah, you can't do that." His face was stone still in the shadows of the cab.

"Do what?"

"Put all your faith in me. I can only do my job to the best of my ability. I can't be your lifeline, and I can't be the object of your faith. I'm just a man."

A lurch rolled in her gut. "What do you mean?"

He rubbed one hand on top of the steering wheel.

"I'm fallible. I make mistakes and . . ." One hand went to his forehead. " . . . Don't make me your savior. I can't be that—to you, or anyone else."

All the tension of the night overcame her. Tears welled as her body shook in tremors.

"You don't understand. Everyone in my life who cared about me is dead." Tears overflowed, but she didn't care. "People look at me and they think I have everything. But I don't. I have money. It doesn't make up for being all alone." She stopped to wipe away the stream of hot liquid on her cheeks. "And now you're telling me I can't count on you, either?"

He reached over and took her hand. The warmth of his touch travelled up her arm.

"Ehvah, you can count on me to provide you with security, and to use my training to protect you. You can count on my friendship. You can count on me being here for you. But I'm a poor substitute for a much greater love. One that will drive away all your fear. I can't compete with that, and I don't want to."

What did he mean? His eyes locked with hers.

"I told you that part of my post-traumatic stress related to my fear of doing something to cause another person's death. I never told you about the event in my life that triggered the fear." He squeezed her hand but kept a firm hold.

"I was on a mission overseas. Intelligence told us the area we were in was deserted, but it wasn't. By the time we discovered there were families living there, it was too late." He looked down at his lap.

"We were ambushed, and a group of civilians were caught in the crossfire between us and our targets. A young boy decided to run across the firing line, and was gunned down. His mother ran out to him and she was also killed."

Ehvah detected his agony in the way his voice faltered.

"Seconds later, another boy—a teenager—ran out to them. By this time both sides had stopped shooting. The boy lay over his family, howling with grief."

David rubbed the back of his neck with his spare hand.

"We maintained our cease-fire, but the other side didn't. They started shooting over the top of the boy. I couldn't stand by while the kid died. We had no clear orders to maintain our positions, so I yelled at my best friend to cover me and I ran out."

A beam of moonlight caught his features. His jawline twitched.

"I got the boy, and pulled him off. We both managed to reach some close cover. I didn't realize until I got to the other side that my mate had come out after me."

He shook his head.

"It all happened so quick. He had distracted the fire that would have hit me and the boy. I got him back behind cover but it was too late."

Ehvah could see his pain. It brought her own losses to the surface. "I can't pretend to understand war, but I do know what it's like to lose someone you love."

"We had about five minutes together before he slipped away. It was the worst five minutes of my life. It was my fault he died. He was the best of us, and my actions killed him. It should have been me."

He closed his eyes for a second.

"I stayed in the army for another year, but I was a mess. I got help, though. Ron Murray was one person who pointed me in the right direction."

Ehvah was stunned by his story.

"But . . . you didn't kill him. How were you to know he was behind you?"

"No my actions didn't kill him but they did put him in danger. He paid the ultimate sacrifice. No greater love exists than to lay down one's life for a friend."

"But you put your life on the line for a complete stranger. You must see the worth in that?"

"I came to see it. Eventually. The chance to use my training to help and protect others was the reason I got into the security business. Once I got a grip on the guilt and fear, I could embrace the positives. But the greatest lesson I learnt was that humanity has serious limitations. We don't hold the keys to life and death. We only dictate where we place our faith."

He squeezed her hand tight.

"You see, God appointed Jesus as the one who holds the keys. Not me. I can't drive out your fear or take away your nightmares any more than a bottle of medication can. In the Bible it says, it is for freedom that Christ has set us free. I truly believe everyone has issues in life that keep them from being free, but we don't have to accept them. A savior already overcame every single one of them for us."

Ehvah bit her lip. His story was a hard one to hear. She thought about her nightmares and the fear inside that drove them.

Can faith set me free?

Something deep inside her told her it could. The same feeling reminded her that she had to come clean. Her lips twitched, forming the confession she needed to make.

"I haven't been entirely honest with you." She looked up at David through wet eyelashes.

"I haven't been entirely honest with anyone, including myself." She took several deep breaths before retelling David every detail of James's murder, from her arrival home, to the dropped earring, the gun shot, the men, and the snake's head on the back of the killer's neck.

"Why didn't you tell the FBI?"

"I don't know." She sighed. "I think I was in shock, and I didn't know what to do. They had exterior footage of the house, so I assumed they knew about it anyway. Mara freaked me out by telling me I was in grave danger, so I clammed up. I guess I thought if I didn't talk about it, it would all go away."

She waited for David's reaction. She expected him to despise her—after all, she hadn't done the right thing—but he didn't say a word. Instead he released her hand and gave the top of it a rub. His touch sent tingles up her arm.

"I have the contact details of the FBI agent who interviewed me. I've decided to call her first thing tomorrow. I know withholding the information was the wrong thing to do."

"It's hard to know what any of us would have done in your situation. Fear can convince us of a lot of bad things. It's not too late to set it to rights."

Ehvah smiled over at him. A mental image of the grey cloud lifting off her head entered her mind.

He offered a smile. The kindness was still there.

David re-started the car and they drove in silence for over two hours before he veered off the main road and onto a dirt track. The new road followed the contours of a mountain range, opening up at a small settlement of houses. Beyond them was a wide creek. Silhouettes of moving water shone in the moonlight.

"Do you have a house here? It's so pretty."

He tilted his head as they travelled down what Ehvah guessed was the main road of the township.

"Not exactly a house."

They pulled into a cleared area. An expanse of sparkling water lay in front of them, and a pier jutted out from the parking space.

Ehvah could see a boat tied to the end of the walkway. It moved in gentle rhythm with the tide.

"Welcome to my humble abode."

David swept his hand towards the pier and exited the car.

***

A dull light streaming from the porthole was the first sign that morning was about to break. Ehvah stretched over the oddly shaped bed to look out the small round window.

A bank of green mangroves lined the opposite side of the creek, and a dull grey sky loomed above. A sea bird flying over the water was the only sign of life.

They had arrived at David's boat well after midnight. It wasn't a great yacht, or an expensive motor cruiser, but an ex-fishing boat. It was difficult to ascertain the full length of the vessel last night, but she had estimated it to be over twenty feet.

There was a large deck at the back, a modest galley, a bathroom on the lower deck adjacent to a set of bunks, and the main cabin where she had slept.

The bed was built into the V-shape of the bow. It was narrow at the head, wide at the foot and just short of queen size, but the mattress was soft, and the gentle rocking had lulled her to sleep.

Ehvah stretched again and reached over to grab her watch. Five-thirty.

She retrieved her journal from her bag and dumped all her thoughts from the previous day down on paper. Her spine tingled as she detailed the way it felt to be held by David, then burst with adrenaline when she retold the attack.

The whistling of a kettle revealed he was also awake.

She shifted to the edge of the bed, pulled her shoes out from underneath, and made her way up into the galley, thankful she had changed into red sweatpants and a t-shirt before bed. A fresh breeze flowed through the back doors of the boat. She stuck her head outside and saw David sitting in a camp chair at the end of the deck.

Their surroundings were as she had pictured the night before. The boat was tied to an old but stable-looking pier. At the end was a cleared area where the rental car was parked. An expanse of mud lay between the water of the creek and the mangroves on the bank. Ehvah recognized rooftops peeking over the trees in the distance.

That must have been the township we passed through.

The musty smell of mangrove mud wafted in with the fresh breeze blowing down the water channel.

David reached for a steaming mug that sat on little table beside him. Ehvah noticed he had his Bible in his lap. He looked over as she walked out.

"Good morning. Feel like a coffee?" He moved to rise.

"Don't get up. I'll get it." She didn't want him to think she was useless, considering their last argument had been over her demanding a drink.

David's smile was broad, leaving no doubt that he was aware of her thoughts.

"There's a cup on the sink. Water's hot."

Ehvah smiled back, hoping that it conveyed her joy at seeing him, and went back inside for the coffee.

When she returned, a seat was set up next to him. She sat down and sipped from the mug.

"How did you sleep?"

His eye looked puffy and sore, but he had iced it down while she had packed, so it was nowhere near the shiner it could have been.

"Amazingly well. I didn't think I would sleep at all. Must have been the rocking."

The steel boat wasn't the luxurious accommodation she was used to, but it had character and charm. This was a vessel that had weathered the ravages of time. It exuded a sense of dependency and assurance. She felt safe, and even more so because she was there with David.

"No nightmares?"

"No, completely dreamless."

She hadn't realized until that moment that her sleep had been so good.

It's because I'm with you.

She wanted to say it aloud, but didn't dare. The last thing she wanted to do was to scare him off. Not now. She rolled her eyes instead.

"It's bad enough that I have nightmares of snakes and death; now I get to add murderous Russians."

David glanced over, a smirk on his face.

"Maybe in your next dream the snake will bite the Russian and he'll drop down dead."

"I can only hope." The concept made her laugh. "What are you reading?" She indicated to the book in his lap.

He opened to the place he had marked.

"Since no man knows the future, who can tell him what is to come? No man has power over the wind to contain it, so no one has power over the day of his death."

He looked up at her. "That author was King Solomon, the wisest man that ever lived."

"I know his story." Ehvah nodded.

David shifted in his chair. He glanced at her before settling his eyes on the shoreline.

"In the last five minutes I spent with my friend as he died, he prayed for me and the boy I had rescued. I think that disturbed me more than anything. I couldn't understand why he didn't he pray for himself."

Ehvah fingered the handle of her cup. David kept his distant focus.

"When I arrived home, I went to see his parents. I knew how devastated they were. They were a close-knit family, but the second I saw his mother she held me tight and said God is good."

He gave her a tight-lipped smile.

"Later I asked her how she could believe that when her son, who had so much faith, had died. She said that if there was one thing she knew for sure, it was that Jesus loved her and her son, and God's love continued on for him as it did for her. She said many times we won't understand why tragedy strikes, but we always have the choice to trust that God's love never ends."

He stopped to pull something out of the front of his Bible and handed it to her. It was a photo of a dark young man standing in front of an old building. A crowd of children swarmed around him.

"That's Amir. He's the boy I rescued. He's a man now. He runs an orphanage, and is also a teacher. Through his faith in Jesus, he was able to forgive the men who killed his family long before I was able to forgive anyone, including myself."

He pointed to the building behind the group in the photo.

"Amir is helping to rebuild his country. He was left an orphan, and yet here he is—the father of many orphans. He's a great example of what trusting in God's love can do."

Ehvah fingered the photo. Amir's smiling face beamed back at her. He was like her—he had lost his family in tragedy, but here he was living a life full of passionate faith.

She recalled what her grandmother had told her when her parents had died. When bad things happen it was hard to trust in God, but even though we don't understand, if we trust in Him, He would give us everything we needed.

It was time to renew her faith in God. It was a faith she had as a child, nurtured by her Gran, but it had been lost along with the passing of her family.

God had never left her. Now she understood that. The night James died, she'd asked God where He was. Well, here He was, right there in her heart where He'd always been.

Jesus, I know you are there. Please help me get over my fear, and lead me to the life I was meant to have. I choose to trust in you. I choose to believe that your love for me will never end, no matter what happens.

As a child she had repeated the prayers taught to her by adults, but this was different. This prayer came from somewhere deep inside her. She felt her heart ache with the words, and tears prick her eyes.

She handed the photo back to David and swallowed before meeting his gaze.

"I'm going to trust that God has a plan for me. Even in all this trouble, I'm not going to worry. I'm leaving it to Him. I'm going to believe that He loves me. Gran always said if I did, He would give me all I needed."

Voicing her decision cemented it in her heart.

David smiled, then reached over to take her hand. His touch sent tingles up her arm.

Movement at the port side broke through their moment. A white-winged bird broke the surface of the water. Ehvah drew a sharp intake at the sight of the wide wingspan.

"Wow."

The bird glided to the bank, its morning catch secure in its curved beak. It settled atop the muddy green branches of the mangrove trees, and rested triumphant over its prey as a squall of wind rippled the surface of the estuary.

"It's a sea eagle." David said. "They're amazing, aren't they?"

"They sure are."

The sight of the bird reminded her of another Bible verse memorized long ago.

Those who hope in the Lord will renew their strength. They will soar on wings like eagles; they will run and not grow weary, they will walk and not be faint.

Ehvah felt a wave of goose bumps from the top of her head to the tips of her toes. Gran would talk about 'God moments'. This had to be one for her. The eagle was a sign.

Perhaps of freedom.

Now everything around her felt like freedom, from the raw beauty of the setting to the spontaneous nature of the vessel.

"How did you come to live here?"

David dropped her hand to settle back in his chair.

"My uncle owned a fleet of these fishing boats. Every school holidays I'd come up and help him on this one. When he died, my cousins sold off the fleet. I bought this boat and some land my uncle owned on an island up north." He leaned back in the camp chair.

"After I left the army, this seemed like a natural place to come to get away from it all. I was pretty messed up."

David pointed to the rooftops of the township.

"Ron and his family live close by. Apart from being a fantastic psychologist, he's also the local church group minister."

"Seriously?" Ehvah smiled.

"Yep. Although I don't think you would call it a church as such, more like a happy group of worshipers. I'm in the band there, too."

"You are full of surprises."

David picked up his mug and flung the dregs into the water.

"So are you. Now, first thing we need to do today is contact that FBI agent."

Ehvah breathed a deep sigh.

Back to reality.

CHAPTER 19

Mara closed her eyes and took a deep breath in an effort to calm the raging surge of anger within. Her conversation with the head of the security agency that morning was bad enough, but now she couldn't reach Lyle. She threw her cell phone into her briefcase. It was all she could do not to grab it and throw it out the window. Better yet, find someone to throw it at.

Its shrill incoming ring made her jump.

"You'd better have some good news for me." She made an effort to control her voice through gritted teeth.

"Unfortunately not." Lyle's voice faltered on the end of the line.

Mara took another deep breath. "Explain."

"The Feds have been into the house and cleared it out. I went through everything that was left. Ehvah's personal stuff was all gone. I told you this was a waste of time. I should have gone straight to the source. It's got to be in something we didn't get out of her hotel room."

Mara could feel the pangs of a tension headache spear her forehead.

"Did you go through her car? The other rooms? The pool house?"

"Of course we did."

"You don't have to use that tone with me." Mara forced a breath out.

"I'm sorry, darling. I've been under a lot of pressure." His voice broke with emotion. "It's been dangerous over here. The FBI is everywhere, my family are not cooperating, and . . ." There was a loud sniff. "We'll just have to go to the beach house and go through everything she has."

"That's impossible. Ehvah's disappeared."

"What do you mean?"

"I had a call from the security company this morning. She's left the beach house and they don't know where she is. She rang in to inform them that she's decided to take an extended holiday and won't be needing their services any more."

"Where's she gone?" Lyle's voice was almost a screech.

"How do I know? Her phone is turned off. I don't know what else to do except keep trying to reach her. But, I swear, when I do . . ."

Mara could feel her head throb as all the violent scenarios played out in her mind.

Heavy breathing on the other end signified that Lyle was in tune with her thoughts. Mara picked up a coffee mug and threw it at the wall. It bounced off the trailer wall without a chip. She couldn't even break a piece of crockery.

"Argh." Her cry of frustration provided no relief. "I can't believe James involved that little tramp. Why? He knew how I felt about her."

There was a pause at the other end before Lyle answered. "I'd say he knew about us."

Mara rolled her eyes. "Of course he knew about us. How could he not?"

"Well, maybe he involved Ehvah to spite you. To get back at us both. Maybe she knows more about this than she's letting on."

Could James have been so calculating? The theory did make sense. Mara had carefully covered her affair with Lyle, but James must have had suspicions—why else would he allude to Lyle in his letter, and involve Ehvah? James was pliable, but he wasn't stupid. Perhaps he also suspected their plan to double-cross him and take the money for themselves.

"Whatever his motivation, it doesn't help us now. I don't think Ehvah knows a thing. She's just making me suffer for controlling her."

Mara thought about the difficult situations she had faced

in her life. She always managed to manipulate and fight her way through. Now was not the time to give up. She couldn't.

"There has to be a way of finding out where James put the money. Even if we have to find Ehvah and beat it out of her."

She rubbed her hand against her bottom lip. "I hate involving your family any further, but I don't see that we have much choice. Get back here as soon as you can."

Lyle didn't wait for her reply before he hung up.

CHAPTER 20

"Here you go."

Ehvah handed over her cell phone.

"Is that everything?"

Agent Gregson's cold blue eyes bore into her as she took the phone.

"Everything I have on me."

Gregson passed the phone to the Australian federal agent accompanying her. Ehvah was shocked to discover he was Phil Smith, the real estate man who had assisted her when she first arrived in the country. The real estate persona was just a cover. It seemed he had been keeping track of her for the FBI since she had arrived.

Phil walked several feet to the end of the back deck and placed the phone in a black case. Her other possessions were in her suitcase which had been transferred from the boat to the pier.

Gregson stayed with them outside the cabin door.

"It was a relief to hear from you yesterday. We were concerned when you disappeared from the beach house. Nice to see you're finally cooperating with us." The disgruntled tone in her voice came through loud and clear.

"I'm sorry. I should have told you everything long before now. I was convinced you would know as much as I did."

Gregson squinted between her and David.

"We do have footage of the suspects, and with some fancy tweaking we identified the snake tattoo. The problem is we don't know who the guy is. Or any of the men he had with him that night. We have strong suspect links to this case, but none of them match the descriptions of the men who killed your uncle. As far as we know, they aren't associated with the Russian crime syndicate."

"Aren't Russian crime gangs known for their tattoos?" David rested one hand on the glass door leading to the cabin.

"Yes. But we haven't seen this particular one before. We can't link it to any particular gang. It's a bit of a mystery." Gregson paused to adjust her sunglasses, then addressed Ehvah. "We've been investigating your uncle and his criminal ties for over six months. We've had surveillance on your property and an informer in the Russian camp, so we knew about the money being transferred. Two days ago, our informer told us about your uncle hiding the location of the money on you."

"I didn't know, I swear." Ehvah shook her head as she spoke.

"I believe you." Gregson's head tilted as she sighed. "We're still trying to piece it all together. Our informer tells us that the Russians didn't kill your uncle and they don't know who did. We need to get all the facts. If we go in prematurely, we risk presenting a weak case that won't hold up."

"How long do you think it will take?" Ehvah could feel a heavy pull in her chest. She closed her eyes and took a deep breath.

"We've been after these guys for too long to let them slip through our fingers now. Our next step is to find the men who shot your uncle, work out how they're involved in the scheme, and, most importantly, find the laundered money. Once those elements are in our hands, the risk to your safety will be minimalized and we'll have an airtight case."

Gregson pointed to the suitcase.

"Hopefully these items you've given me will hold the key. We've pulled apart your home in the US but found nothing."

She gave Ehvah another direct glare. "You can't think of anywhere your uncle would have hidden the details of the bank account on you?"

Ehvah had been racking her brain, trying to think where James would have stashed the information. "I have no idea.

Unless it's in one of those items."

Her entire existence was in her suitcase. Gregson had demanded she surrender every piece of clothing she had with her, even the new items she had purchased in Australia. They demanded that everything she owned be thoroughly checked.

Gregson didn't shift her gaze. Ehvah felt her heart beat a little faster under the scrutiny of the astute woman. From the moment the American agent had arrived, Ehvah had felt like an amoeba under a microscope.

She pulled on the bottom of David's shirt that she was wearing. She didn't have to worry about its length covering her. It fell just short of her knees, longer than any miniskirt she had ever worn.

David stood beside her.

"What happens now? Is there some sort of witness protection program available until you can wrap this up?"

"That's not an option. We can't offer that here in Australia due to the nature of the situation. And even if you did travel back the States, the investigation is yet to fit that criteria because we don't have any firm suspects for the murder."

Phil nodded, confirming his colleague's assessment.

"At this point, it's vital that you're somewhere safe, and that we are able contact you at all times. I don't anticipate it will be long before we have a breakthrough. We're closing in."

Gregson moved several paces towards the back of the boat before turning around.

"We have a lot of people working on this, both here and back in the States, but not knowing the location is slowing us up considerably. Fact is, your uncle was very good at moving money around. And very good at covering his tracks."

"I'm going to pay your aunt a visit." Gregson crossed her arms.

"Why?"

"We've always suspected she's had some involvement but we've never had any hard evidence linking her to what your uncle was doing. The fact that she discouraged you from talking to us tells me something's up. This case is a lot bigger than you think. This particular faction has been laundering money through organizations like your uncle's for years."

"I think you're right. She has something to do with it," David said.

Ehvah looked up to see a deep frown on David's face.

"I know a place I can take her. I'll give your man all the details." He indicated to Phil who grabbed a notebook and pen from his pocket as David met him at the back of the boat.

Gregson gave her a tight smile.

"I'm sorry, but you'll just have to weather this through. You have security in place already and that's a better situation than anything I could offer you. I'll keep you posted, and call me immediately if you think of something, or there's any further contact."

With that, both agents exited the boat.

Phil reached down and offered David his card. He gave Ehvah a wink.

"Hang in there. We've got a lot of people on this."

Ehvah tried to smile, but she could barely manage a slight turn at the corners of her mouth.

As the agents made their way down the jetty, Ehvah felt a chill at the thought of the violence these men could inflict. A sick feeling swelled in her stomach and she closed her eyes tight.

Please, God, help us. Don't let them come after me again.

A warm hand slipped over hers, forcing her eyes back open. David looked down at her for a second before pulling her to him. Ehvah allowed her body to lean in, while her heart beat in her ears.

"It'll all be okay. I'll do everything I can to protect you."

She melted into him, pulling her body hard against his. His chest wasn't the rock-like surface it looked to be. It was warm, and the heavy beating of his heart fed her strength. His embrace enveloped her, making her feel like this was the safest place in the world.

Between the strength of his arms and the power of her prayer, for once it felt like she wasn't facing life alone.

CHAPTER 21

"It feels good to be wearing the right size clothing again."

Ehvah breathed a sigh of contentment for the comfortable sweatpants. The soft pink material covered her thighs and fell down around her feet. Fake rhinestones dotted the sides of the legs. They were a little gaudy, but still complimented the casual outfit. She inspected her reflection in the full length mirror.

"Are you certain you won't need these clothes?" she asked the teenage girl behind her.

The girl screwed up her cute upturned nose. "Nope. I've only worn them a few times. They're too good for around here anyway."

Ehvah smiled back at the reflection.

Rhianna—Rhi—was Dr. Murray's sixteen-year-old daughter. She was gorgeous, with a mass of dark curly hair, chocolate brown eyes, a slim physique, and a sweet countenance to match her physical attractiveness.

She had also been kind enough to lend Ehvah some of her clothing, now that the FBI had taken every possession she owned.

Ehvah rotated to face her.

"As soon as I can, we'll go shopping together in the city and you can pick out whatever you want. A whole new wardrobe on me. I promise."

She shared her best smile with her new young friend.

"That is so kind of you, but I'll probably just buy a heap of shorts and t-shirts. It's the standard dress around here. We don't go anywhere flash." Rhi bit her bottom lip.

Ehvah touched the top of her arm.

"I'll talk to your Mom and Dad. Maybe they'll let me take you somewhere nice, like a restaurant or the theatre or something."

Rhi's eyes widened. "That would be so cool. You are so nice, nothing like they say."

The mention of "they" sent Ehvah's spirits into a nosedive. No doubt Rhi was referring to the tabloids and society bloggers.

"They don't know me. I'm not perfect, but I am human."

She sighed and began to fold the other items Rhi had given her. Ehvah could tell that the girl had offered up her best. Several times she had forced down grateful tears in the presence of the teenager's generosity, and had vowed to give back tenfold.

"I'm sorry. I shouldn't have mentioned the bad stuff."

Ehvah could see remorse in her new friend's eyes.

"It's okay. Whatever happens, I'm putting my past behind me. I have to concentrate on the future." Just saying the words made her feel powerful.

"Does that future include Dave?" Rhi raised her eyebrows. "You know, if you had come a few months ago, I would have been super jealous of you. Dave is such a spunk. I had the biggest crush on him for a while."

Ehvah couldn't help but grin as Rhi bounced cross-legged on the bed. She found the edge and joined her.

"How long have you known David?" she asked.

"In some way or another, my whole life."

Ehvah could see that the girl had a great deal of respect for the security guard.

"I've only known him a month and a bit. I didn't even know he lived on a boat."

That revelation had been a complete surprise to Ehvah, and she wondered what more she didn't know about David.

"He would come here all the time when he was a kid, but I wasn't born then." Rhi picked up one of the stuffed toys that adorned her bed. "He was here all the time visiting Dad until about six months ago. I know he had some kind of post-traumatic stress. I asked Dad about it once. He told me it was a hard thing to go through. Dave always came across as a tough guy, but inside he was hurting."

Rhi squeezed the pink giraffe she was cuddling. "Don't take this the wrong way . . ." She stopped to peek up under her lashes. " . . . but you won't hurt him . . . will you?"

The question came with a heartfelt delivery that almost annihilated Ehvah.

"No. Of course I won't."

There was too much force in her reply, but she was taken aback by Rhi's directness.

If anyone is going to get hurt here, it'll be me.

The thought gave her goose bumps, and her heart told her it was accurate.

"I'm sorry if I was a bit rude, but it's just that Dave's like family to us. He's a special guy and he deserves the best." Rhi stopped to reach out and touch her arm. "Not that you aren't the best, but you are super sophisticated and crazy beautiful, not to mention rich and famous, so it looks a little like heartbreak stuff to me."

Ehvah took a moment to process the girl's comment. To the outside eye they would look like a disastrous match. Anyone who had read a recent tabloid, or taken an interest in celebrity news, would see that she came across as a complete and utter mess.

No wonder Rhi thinks I'm a disaster waiting to happen.

Historically, and figuratively, she was.

Maybe I am, Lord. Maybe he is far better off without me.

Ehvah looked away in an effort to ward off the pain her inner voice aroused in her heart.

Rhi must have picked up on her distress because she uncrossed her legs and shifted closer.

"Hey, don't listen to me. I could be wrong. You're so different in person to anything I've ever read. And Dad loves you. He's, like, your biggest fan. And he's never seen your show. He hasn't even listened to any of your songs."

Ehvah had to smile at Rhi's animated face as she spoke about her father's lack of Ehvah Rowe knowledge.

"He does like your parents' music though." Her face froze, eyes wide and mouth open. "Oh, man, I shouldn't have mentioned them either."

Her countenance fell so dramatically from happy to horrified that the contrast was comical. She hit her forehead with the palm of one hand.

Ehvah burst out laughing at the roller coaster ride of teenage awkwardness.

"You must think I'm a complete idiot. Do you hate me?" Rhi's mouth drooped along with her eyelids.

Ehvah placed a loose arm around the girl's shoulders and gave her a squeeze. "No. I think you're brave and honest. I admire you for being concerned for David. Especially when he's like family to you."

"It's just that . . . " Rhi paused to take a breath. " . . . he had a horrible ex. I mean, she was a real piece of work. She came across all nice and stuff, but she was mean. She was pretty and wore lots of expensive clothes, but when it came to supporting Dave, she was never there."

Ex?

Rhi threw the giraffe back into the stack of stuffed toys located in the corner of the bed. "I know he was relieved when she left, but I don't want that to happen to him again."

Ehvah admired the girl's tenacity. It must have taken a lot of courage to voice her opinion.

"Don't worry. I have a feeling if anyone ends up with a broken heart it will be me." Ehvah bobbed her head and rolled her eyes in an attempt to downplay the all-too-true statement.

Rhi smiled.

Ehvah was relieved to see that she had bought her flippancy act.

"I know what you mean. He is pretty hot, hey?"

Ehvah managed a genuine smile.

"So you said you used to have a crush on David. Anyone special take his place?"

Ehvah delighted in Rhi's widened eyes and over-zealous retelling of the attributes of her newfound crush—a young seventeen-year-old called Brady.

CHAPTER 22

David grabbed the bags of supplies from Ron.

"Thanks."

"Do you know how long you'll be away?" Ron swung a leg over the side of the boat and onto the back deck.

"Not sure. Depends how long it takes for them to get a breakthrough in the case." David stowed the bags inside the galley door before joining his friend at the back of the boat.

"Is Ehvah still over at your place?"

Ron smiled wide.

"Sure is. She and Rhianna are locked in the bedroom, trying on clothes. There was a lot of giggling coming from in there when I left."

The thought of the girls enjoying each other's company made him smile.

"Rhi'll take her mind off it all for a bit."

Ron nodded.

"This has been an enormous shock. I'm surprised she hasn't had a meltdown. She's a little toughie, but this is whole new level of stress."

David took a seat and relayed the events just past where Ehvah had revealed she was trusting God to see her though. "That's going to be the breakthrough that counts," he finished.

"I'll be praying for you both." Ron's smile widened. He stood to leave.

He made a move over the side of the boat and up onto the jetty.

"I'll go and get her. No doubt my family have smothered her long enough. You look after her." He presented a hand back over the side.

"Count on it." David gripped firm.

"God's speed, my friend." Ron dropped his hand.

David watched as he walked back down the pier. He thought about Ron's words. It was up to him to look after Ehvah. A pang of anguish pierced his chest. How could he distance himself from her enough to do that? Since finding out the gravity of the situation, the protective elements of his nature had intensified. He felt them morphing with the attraction he had for her. It was a dire combination—especially when he had a job to do. Leaving her for a short time with Ron's family had been almost impossible for him. He could feel his connection to her growing stronger every second they spent together. And there was nothing he could do about it.

He closed his eyes, feeling the boat sway under his feet.

Lord, help me get this all in perspective of your plan. How can I be of any use if I focus on her instead of the job?

He didn't know what was to come, but at least he knew they wouldn't walk the path alone.

***

Mara squinted hard against the sunlight that flowed in through the glass doors of the beach house.

"Are you certain I can't get you something? Coffee?"

FBI agent Gregson raised her thin brows. Mara sucked in a sharp breath as cold eyes bore through her.

"No, thank you. This won't take long," the agent said.

Mara seated herself in a chair across the table from her unwanted guest.

"To be honest, I don't know why you're here. I made my statement back home. Nothing's changed. Are you gathering more information on my husband's murder?"

Gregson drummed her fingertips on the table. The soft clacking broke the noise of the ocean beyond the veranda doors.

"I understand your niece has been staying in this house. Is she still here?"

Mara scanned the agent's stony features. She gave

nothing away. Why was she in Australia?

"Ehvah came here to recuperate after her traumatic experience back home. I don't know where she is now. She disappeared before I arrived, which was two days ago. She didn't leave any contact details."

Why was this agent here now? Did they know she was involved? Were they closing in on them? Mara pushed down the simmering explosion of confusion and fear within. It wouldn't be wise for the agent to see her rattled.

"You're not in contact with your niece?"

Mara let out a dramatic harrumph. "I'm not her keeper. Ehvah does what she wants. She always has."

"She didn't speak to you about your husband's murder while she was here?"

Mara tilted her chin and gazed into the distance, making a poignant effort to look contemplative.

"Not that I recall. We don't have a close relationship."

Gregson lifted one eyebrow. "Yet it's close enough for you to organize this holiday house for her. Close enough for you to convince her to follow you here."

Mara expelled her breath so hard her nostrils flared.

"Agent Gregson, it's no secret that my niece and I have a strained relationship. But we are still family. We're the only family each other has left. I feel a sense of loyalty to her, in spite of our differences. Is she in some sort of trouble that I should know about? Is that why you're here?"

The agent lowered her eyebrow and twitched her nose. Her focus remained steady.

Mara could feel the tension hanging thick in the air. She concentrated on maintaining eye contact with the formidable woman. If she broke away it would be a sign she was hiding something. She drew on all her training as an actress and focused on the game.

A wind gust outside forced Gregson to blink. She wet her lips in slow motion.

"I'm afraid I can't discuss the case any further. I think I'm done here." She stood from the table and pushed her chair in. "Call us if you have any contact with your niece."

She slipped a card onto the table.

Mara reviewed it, racking her brain for a way to get more information out of the woman.

"Why are you here in Australia? I'd like to know if there's been some sort of development in my husband's murder case." If she could find out how much the FBI knew, it could also reveal how much time she had left.

"Our presence here is classified." Gregson readjusted her tailored suit. "Just know we're closing in."

Mara felt a tremor in her hands. She wasn't sure if it was inspired by fear, or adrenaline, or a mixture of both. She saw the agent to the door and closed it firm behind her, then leaned back against the timber and closed her eyes. Several months earlier she had reveled in the fact she had everything she wanted. Money, a revived career, and men she could control. Now it felt as though her life was on course to mirror the pathetic tragedy that was her mother.

Her heart beat hard, and her forehead began to bead with sweat. She pulled her focus back to the task of regaining control.

"There's still time."

She had to do whatever it took to get what was hers.

CHAPTER 23

"I don't know if these were the best choice!" Ehvah looked down at the high-waisted hot pants she was wearing. On Rhi's girlish frame they had appeared modest, but on her body she suspected they became what they were meant to be: hot.

David looked up from the wheel of the boat to give her a lopsided smile.

"I liked seeing you in my flannel shirts, but I have to admit, this is a little better-fitting."

Ehvah felt a jump in her stomach. When he smiled, little creases formed around his eyes, making his rugged appearance even more desirable. She smiled back, hoping that the emotion reached her eyes just as it did his.

"I did like your flannel shirts, but it was good of Rhi to let me borrow so much of her wardrobe. And give me some toiletries." Ehvah already missed her connection with Dr. Murray's youngest daughter.

"She's a good girl." David reached out to fiddle with the controls of the boat as they powered through the estuary.

"She told me she used to have a huge crush on you." Ehvah couldn't help but giggle at the young girl's confession.

David gave her a stony look.

"What do you mean, 'used to'?"

"You have been usurped by a seventeen-year-old hottie at youth group. Rhi tells me he's much better looking than you are."

"Women are so fickle." He shook his head in mock disgust.

"She's one of the most together sixteen-year-olds I've

ever come across."

Ehvah looked out the back to see a fish jump in the boat's wake, right next to the little dinghy they were towing.

"I envy her a little. She's so innocent and happy. When I was fifteen I had a sitcom, a singing career, and a whole lot of emotional baggage stuffed down deep inside just waiting to burst out. It looked like I had everything, but all I remember was getting up in the morning and thinking I had to keep working, that if I kept working, I'd be alright."

Spending the time with Rhi had evoked conflicting emotions. On one hand, Ehvah was delighted to be with someone so vibrant, but on the other hand, Rhi's life reminded her of what she had missed out on.

"Is that why you partied so hard for a while there?" David took his eyes off the channel for a moment to connect with hers.

Ehvah nodded.

"When the show ended, I didn't have work to fall back on. I needed something to fill my time. And maybe I never had anyone around me who understood what trauma was, or how to deal with it. It's my own fault too, I always looked like I was handling everything so well."

"People who are strong by nature are easily overlooked when it comes to experiencing trauma. They tend to grit their teeth and stick it out, but it comes through eventually." David readjusted the cap he was wearing before continuing.

"I suspect we have that in common. I think my faith has driven home to me that there's a season for everything. If we skip a season, or spend too much time in one, we miss out. For me, allowing myself to feel the pain was just as important as working through it."

Oh my.

"I hear that. I never grieved my parents properly, then I threw myself into work after Gran died. With James, I ran away as fast as I could. I still can't believe I let Mara convince me to do that. The one smart thing I've done is to get help from people who care. Like you and Dr. Murray."

David glanced over and gave her a reassuring smile.

Ehvah leaned back against the counter and looked out

the galley window as they fell into comfortable silence. The afternoon sun was softening in the sky and the drum of the engine flowed in rhythmic motion with the lapping of breaking water on the bow.

"Rhi told me about your last girlfriend. I'm sorry it didn't work out." She cringed at the absurdity of her words. "Well, not that sorry. Just that it sounded like a pretty bad breakup."

Not much better.

David's mouth tilted up at the corners signaling his amusement at her awkward choice of words.

"Breakups are never fun, but it was for the best. My experiences in combat changed me. I wasn't the same person she knew before. Sometimes relationships can survive that and become even stronger. We couldn't."

He touched the wheel as he spoke, making slight corrective moves in motion with the swell.

"She couldn't understand how I felt, and she didn't want to. I couldn't go back to the way I was before. Not for her or anyone."

He stopped to let a deep sigh escape.

"As much as those experiences changed me for the worse, knowing the Lord has turned every trauma in my life around for my good."

Her eyes connected with his.

"My father would say that all the time—that his life was a series of bad choices that God turned around for his good." Ehvah sighed at the memory.

"Well, for me there's no therapy in the world that beats handing it all over to God. It hasn't been easy. There's been no quick fix. It's been heart wrenching, but so worth it." David gave her a smile.

He reached over to increase the throttle, sending the engine into a vibrant burble.

"That relationship ended over a year ago. It seems like a lifetime."

Ehvah felt a wave of relief. Rhi's comments about David's previous relationship had sent her imagination into overload. Now it was clear that David wasn't carrying any regrets over the breakup.

Just remember what she said about you not being any better.

Rhi's words echoed in her brain.

"Looks like heartbreak stuff to me."

Was she right? Ehvah grabbed the side of the galley counter and steadied herself against the gentle sway of the boat.

God, I want to be with this man so bad, but I don't want to hurt any more, and I don't want him to hurt any more either. I'm tired of being hurt and sad and lonely. I'm tired of being scared and always running from something. From now on, I'm running to you, and if David is a part of that, then please show us. If he isn't, I'll accept that too. However hard that will be.

"Not long to go now." David pointed out the windscreen, indicating to the right of the boat. "This side is the mainland. And this side is an island, a big one." He gestured to the left. "We're in the channel between the two. It's about fifty kilometers long. The largest section's a kilometer wide."

Ehvah had noticed a heavy swell rising now they were in deeper waters, but it was probably a calm ride compared to the open ocean.

He pointed to the right where a creek snaked off into the mangroves. "All these little creeks feed into the estuary. There's a lot of them. We came from one of the larger ones."

"So where are we going?" It didn't look as though they were heading anywhere near civilization.

"See that smaller island up there in the middle of the channel?"

She pointed to the distant green. "That one?"

"Yep. Just past that. Then there'll be a bit of walking."

"Just as well Rhi gave me some sneakers then."

She looked out the back of the boat in time to see another fish splash behind them. "I'm going out for a moment."

David gave her a nod.

A salt spray engulfed her as she stepped out the door. The grey morning clouds had vanished and the sun shone warm against her bare forearms. A squall whipped her hair around her face. Little openings in the mangroves broke the masses of water plants each side of them, and the island presented a formidable rainforest stretching far up into the sky.

As Ehvah sat and watched the dinghy skip over their wake, the occasional sea bird would appear, squawking above the noise of the engine. The fresh scent of the ocean morphed with the odd waft of the boat's bilge.

An enormous blue butterfly found its way onto the deck. Its wings were so blue they looked as though they had been painted on. It was joined by another, then another, and another, each flying off as quickly as they had arrived, and all heading in the same direction.

I wonder where they're going, and why don't their wings get tired?

Ehvah made a mental note to ask David.

Even if she wasn't the girl for him, he could still be her friend. She vowed not to let anything get in the way of that.

***

"Are you sure your cousin is the right person to help us?" Mara clicked her pen in and out as she spoke. Her desperation was affecting her nerves.

"He's the best in the business, and the only person I trust. We'll have to cut him in, though. I named a price," Lyle answered on other end of the phone line.

Mara swallowed hard.

"Well, you're both here in Australia now. You'd better get the first flight out of Brisbane and up here to find her."

As much as Mara hated involving Lyle's family, she had run out of options. They were no closer to finding the money, and now they couldn't find Ehvah. Every second counted. Both the Russians and the FBI would be on the hunt for the money, so the sooner they found it and disappeared, the better.

"How's the beach house?" Lyle asked.

"It's cooler than the swamp I was in, but I'm still stuck in the middle of nowhere." Mara stopped to close the curtain, as if blocking out the tropical scene would make all her problems go away.

"The production company want me out of the house now that Ehvah isn't here to pay for it, but I'm holding on for now. I've been told some of my scenes have been cut. At this point I don't care. I just want to find my money and get out of here."

It was looking as if her comeback role would also be her swan song. There was no doubt that the stress of the situation had affected her acting ability, and not for the better. The director had chastised her for her lack of professionalism and talent several times.

Just another thing to thank Ehvah for.

The future looked bad for her career. The money was now her only hope for a comfortable life. Either that, or be destined for the same life as her mother—submitting to men for a meal ticket, each and every choice stealing a little more of her power and self-esteem.

That wasn't going to be her destiny.

"We'll put your cousin to work. He had better find what we're looking for."

"Don't worry, he will. He has no qualms employing whatever tactics are necessary. He scares me."

"Everything scares you, Lyle." She rolled her eyes.

"We'll do what we need to."

CHAPTER 24

David checked the mooring one last time. With big tides forecast over the next week it was imperative that the boat was secure.

He picked his way around the edge of the vessel towards the stern to meet Ehvah. She was standing at the edge of the deck with the backpack he had told her to fill sitting at her feet. Her black shorts and pink t-shirt were girly, but somehow the clothes made her look older and more desirable.

Wisps of blonde hair fell out from the ponytail under her cap, drawing David's eye to her long slender neck. She shifted her weight as she looked over the side, one hip jutting out a little more than the other. The movement produced a perfect contour, inspiring an undeniable stirring inside him.

Got it bad.

He rolled his eyes at the thought. He did have it bad, but he had to rein it in. This wasn't the time or place to be stoking a flaming desire. If the situation was bad before, now it was worse. There was no way a relationship would work under the circumstances. Wisdom told him to get some control, which was in complete contrast to what his heart was telling him—to find some courage and go for it. Each time he touched her it confirmed that he was falling in love with her, and that was something he couldn't let happen.

He sighed as he stepped down onto the deck.

"All ready?"

Her huge emerald eyes acknowledging him with warmth. His stomach did a flip.

I am in so much trouble.

She licked her lips.

"Yep. I'm all set. I didn't think it was possible for me to travel so light. If I still had a phone, I'd take a photo of this." She picked up the backpack and handed it to him.

"Just goes to show how little we can live on." He took it from her and pulled on the tow rope, drawing the little dinghy to the edge.

"You know, I've been thinking the exact same thing. At home I have a house full of stuff, yet here I am Down Under having the best time, with not one personal possession."

"The best time hiding from a pack of criminals?" David climbed over the side of the boat and into the tinny.

Ehvah giggled. "That does sound crazy, but I can honestly say that I haven't felt this happy for a long time. It must have something to do with the company." She smiled as she reached out and took the hand he offered. "In L.A., it's all about who you are, what you look like, how much you make—popularity and status. In my circle, anyway. It's exhausting, and nothing ever feels real."

David tried to help her into the dinghy. She sat on the boat's thick timber railing, shifting weight several times in an effort to reach one foot into the boat. The rise and fall of both boats made a gentle reach impossible.

"Here!"

He let go of her hand and got a good grip on her waist, pulling her down into the smaller boat with ease. He kept her close for a moment while she grew accustomed to the vigorous movement of the smaller vessel. He was just about to let her go when she looked him square in the face. For a second if felt as though the entire earth stood still. She filled his senses from the curve of her body under his hands to the scent of her floral perfume that carried along the salt breeze, from her cute cap to her full pink lips. Lips he was now struggling not to kiss.

To his complete surprise, it was Ehvah who pulled away from him. She scrambled to settle onto the front bench.

It wasn't the first time David acknowledged he had dodged a bullet. From now on any close physical contact with her had to be kept to a minimum.

What where we talking about?

He racked his brain for a continuation of their conversation.

Fake people?

"Pleasure seekers," he said while pulling on the outboard cable. The motor sprang to life.

"What do you mean?"

He spun back to face her as he revved the outboard and pulled the tinny away from the boat.

"My grandfather calls them pleasure seekers. People whose goal in life is to seek the next pleasurable thing or experience. He reckons some spend their entire existence devoted to it. My Pop can be a philosopher at times, not to mention a bit direct." He felt a smile tilt up the corners of his mouth. "He used to refer to my ex as a pleasure seeker. He was right."

There's another dodged bullet.

Ehvah held the edge of the seat as they skipped over the water.

"That's exactly the sort of people I hung out with. People who devoted their entire lives to seeking pleasure. I guess a lot of them would say there's nothing wrong with that. But they never seemed to be happy, even when they had everything. I have everything and I wasn't happy. Your Pop sounds like an honest man."

David shook his head.

"He's honest alright. You're about to discover that for yourself."

CHAPTER 25

Ehvah stopped to catch her breath. Their walk had started in paradise, down on a white sandy beach, and had ended in no-man's-land on top of a mountainous range. She balanced her footing and looked back. The winding track stretched down the hillside through a thicket of shrubbery and trees. Glimpses of the yellow beach below signified just how far they had climbed.

"You alright?" David asked from a few feet ahead.

Ehvah was too exhausted to talk. She placed one hand on her hip and rested on the large stick David had given her to help stabilize her footing.

"Please tell me . . ." She paused to suck in some air. "Tell me it's not much further."

David grinned at her. "It's not much further."

He didn't seem out of breath at all.

"Here, sit down for a minute." He indicated a large rock on the side of the track.

Ehvah didn't hesitate, securing her stick and taking a seat on the flattest section of the rock. It had occurred to her several times as they climbed the hill that she had to do something about her fitness, but she was determined not to voice her inadequacies aloud. The single indication David was working hard was the sweat patch she could see forming on the back of his shirt.

"You're doing great." He took a seat on the ground beside her.

"I'm not." She took the water bottle he offered.

"Trust me, you're doing fine. I've seen a lot of people struggle harder than you on this walk. It isn't much further.

About one hundred meters to the top, then the country changes to rainforest trekking. It's cooler, and flatter."

Ehvah handed him the bottle and looked out to the twisting blue and green channel below. A massive creek maze covered the distance between the island and the mainland. It was so vibrant that it looked like a living, breathing thing.

"At least the view is worth it." Ehvah couldn't recall seeing anything like it. "What did you say this island was called?"

"Hinchinbrook. It's one of the largest islands on the coast, but runs close to the mainland." He pointed to a large mountainous area on the distant mainland. "That's Cardwell Range. The estuary runs right up to the base of those mountains."

Ehvah measured the distance between where the mangroves started on the opposite bank to where the range was.

"That's awesome. You mean there are creeks all through there?"

"As far as you can see." David lifted his cap to rub his damp hair.

"It's so beautiful."

Ehvah felt mesmerized by the sun that sparkled on the water below. Her trance was broken by a movement between the rock and David. A slimy looking creature about eight inches long slithered across the ground. It's curvy, flat-bellied progression made her jump and scream.

"Snake." She pointed to the creature.

David looked down and removed his sunglasses. To her horror he reached out and touched its back.

"It's not a snake, it's a legless lizard. See its little ear holes and these tiny little legs?" He flipped the creature over and pointed to a growth jutting out from the body.

"How can they be legs?" Ehvah couldn't fathom how the lizard would walk on them.

"It doesn't use them any more, but it's still a lizard, even though it looks like a snake. These guys don't have any venom, or a forked tongue. Don't ever touch one though, just in case. There are snakes here. We've had a few get into the camp. Mostly carpet snakes."

Ehvah felt a wave of hot terror stream though her body. "Tell me you're kidding."

David secured his hat and stood up. He shuffled his feet in the dirt and looked like he was going to say more, but instead he retrieved her stick, holding it out for her.

"You'll be right. If you see one, hold this stick at lengthways between you and the snake."

"But what if I don't see it and it bites me?"

"Watch where you're walking so you will see it. Don't worry, they're more afraid of you than you are of them. The real ones are easier to handle than the ones in your dreams. For the most part, the real ones will get out of your way, but if you have any trouble yell coo-ee. I promise I'll come running."

The plan didn't put her mind at ease.

"Coo-ee?" It seemed like a strange thing to yell. Why not yell 'help'?

David cupped his hands together, tilted into the air, and called, "Cooooo-eeeee." The sound echoed off the mountains and into the channel below.

"Like that. It's what the bushmen in Australia yell when they want to find each other. It can be our emergency signal in case you need me. You try."

Ehvah cupped her hands and tilted her head back just as he had.

"Cooooooo-eeeeee." Her call reverberated around them.

"You've got a great set of lungs." David gave her a broad smile.

"All the vocal training, probably." Ehvah laughed.

His hand brushed hers as she reached out to take the stick from him. An electric current streamed through her arm at his touch. Over the last few days, Ehvah had noticed that her physical reactions to him had grown much stronger. The flutter in her belly had morphed into a full-on lurch, and the tingle at his touch now sent her nerves into spasms.

There was no doubt David was aware of her attraction to him. She cringed when she recalled the pathetic way she had all but begged him to stay with her and take her around Australia. Now, after her conversation with Rhi, she wondered if her presence in his life was destructive. Rhi was right—the last thing David needed was more trouble, and right now she came with a whole load of it.

It would have been much easier for him to walk away, or get someone else to look after her security, but he didn't. He stuck by her. She made a new vow to appreciate his friendship and keep her feelings under control.

But he didn't make it easy when he looked at her the way he was now, gaze fixed on her, a smile that reached his eyes, and a body close enough for her to reach out and touch.

The lurch in her belly forced her to look away. She tapped the end of her stick into the dirt.

Why doesn't he just kiss me and get it over with?

The thought sent nervous energy corseting through her body from the top of her head to the tips of her toes.

Say something.

"Um, so, are there spiders here too?" She looked up to find him securing the water bottle in the backpack.

"Heaps. Why? Are you afraid of them?"

Ehvah cringed. "I'm not phobic or anything, but I can't say I'm a fan of eight-legged critters."

David flung the pack onto his back.

"Well, just check your shoes before you put them on." His big grin suggested he was teasing.

"Yeah, right!" She started off ahead of him, but he caught her in a few steps.

"No, seriously. Check your shoes." With that he marched out in front.

Lizards that look like snakes, actual snakes, and now spiders. Great.

Ehvah took some satisfaction in the thought that avoiding contact with unspeakable creatures would redirect her energy away from falling in love with David.

***

The sound of a car pulling into the driveway forced Mara

from her position on the veranda. She made her way through the beach house and out to the side in time to see Lyle and his cousin exit the rental car.

"What did you find out?"

Lyle pressed the lock before answering.

"We think she's with one of the security men who were here looking after her."

Mara gave a loud, "Humph. Figures. Little tart."

Vinnie, Lyle's cousin, sidled up to her. Mara shot him her best disgusted look. Like Lyle, Vinnie was of average height, with Mediterranean features. But that was where the similarities ended. Vinnie was heavyset and shared none of Lyle's personal grooming habits. He was slovenly, dirty, and—in the heightened humidity of Cairns—smelly.

"How did you find this out?" Mara asked.

"How do you think?" Vinnie said in an untamed Jersey slur. "We acted like we was all worried about her and the guy at the security company slipped up. Said something about her being in good hands."

Mara felt a fresh wave of displeasure at the presence of the man beside her.

If only we could do this without involving the scum.

She bit her tongue so she wouldn't voice her thoughts. Right now they needed Vinnie.

"I knew that security man would be more talkative if I sent you. We have ten days to find her and get the information we need. I convinced the production company to give me an extension on this house, but after that they expect me back at the studio in L.A."

"Did the FBI show up again?" Lyle placed a peck on her cheek.

"No. But we don't have a lot of time."

"We asked around the shops near the security place." Vinnie stopped to light a cigarette. "One lady at a coffee shop told us the security guy has a place up north, on the water."

He handed her a napkin with a name scribbled on it.

Lyle and Vinnie shared a look Mara couldn't interpret.

"We've got a plan."

CHAPTER 26

"It's a bit rugged."

David knew it was the understatement of the year. In a few minutes the camp would be in sight, and his exaggeration would become obvious.

"I haven't always lived in luxury, you know." Ehvah's breathing was heavy behind him as they trekked their way through a dense section of rainforest. "When I was a child, my parents were always touring. We'd go from tour buses to hotel rooms. Some were pretty rough, especially in the early days."

He stopped and waited for her to secure her footing after climbing over a large tree root.

"Sometimes the tour would stop at a campsite off the highway. There'd be open fires, s'mores, and the entire band would get out their instruments and have this big acoustic jam session, right in the middle of nowhere. All the other campers would sit around and have a sing-along. It was the best time." Her voice conveyed a whimsical response to the memory.

"Sounds like great fun."

She looked up from under the brim of her cap. "It was some of the best times I can remember."

He resumed a steady pace along the path.

"This one time, I must have been about ten, or close to it, we stopped at this place in Texas. It was the darkest night and the stars in the sky were amazing. Mom and Dad were singing together. Just them, not the rest of the band. I looked over and I thought my Mom looked like an angel. Must have been the campfire light. Sometimes, when I miss her, I'll close my eyes and see her just as she was that night."

There was a slight pause in her voice before she continued.

"She was so beautiful. I think that's why I get a bit angry when people tell me I look like her. Not that I mind the comparison in a physical sense, but it's just that to me, she was an exquisite angel. Nobody will ever remember her the way I do."

David stopped to look back at her. With the sea breeze flying wisps of hair around her face she had the look of a celestial being herself.

"I think you look like you. A beautiful, unique you." He hoped his smile would do something to assure her of the honesty his words.

She cocked her head to the side and flashed him a devastating smile.

"I think that may have been the nicest compliment anyone has ever paid me." She bit her lip and played with the end of her stick.

He was almost overwhelmed by an urge to pull her to him. His hands twitched with the longing for it and his arms stiffened, ready to do the bidding of his heart. He took a step forward, the intention to hold her firmly rooted in his body as well as in his mind.

"Hoy, lad. Is that you?"

The voice at the end of the path was accompanied by the sound of a dog barking.

"Hey Pop," he called. "Ready to meet my grandfather? He lives here permanently and takes care of the place for me." He turned back to Ehvah. "He's a bit of a cranky old codger." He could tell from her bemused expression that she didn't understand what he had said.

"A mad old man." He interpreted his Australian expression for her. "You just give as good as you get."

She smiled. "How bad can he be?"

David waited until she couldn't see him to roll his eyes.

Lord, please keep Pop in check.

Prayer was all he had when it came to his grandfather's temperament.

***

The forest track gave way to a cleared area as they followed Pop's voice through the trees. Ehvah trod carefully, still conscious of the nasty creatures that David told her inhabited the island. It wasn't that she was petrified of them, more that she preferred not to personally run into any of them. Especially the snakes.

She looked up as they entered the flat area.

A wide grassed plateau spread out to her right. At the end of it was a view to die for. Cardwell Range, the mountainous region on the mainland David had pointed out earlier, was prominent in the distance. A honeycomb-like estuary spread across the foreground.

Ehvah stopped for a moment, consumed by the sight. Amalgamated blues and greens cast a brilliant blanket of color that expanded as far as her eye could see. It was almost as if a graphic artist had artificially airbrushed the entire scene.

At the far end of the cleared area was a structure that looked a bit like a garage, but bigger. It was made of tin, and there was an assortment of paraphernalia at the side, including a few canvas chairs, a table, something that looked like a steel barrel on legs, and a garden at the edge of the mountain.

A sweet scent of an unknown native flower wafted her way, accompanied by the musty scent of campfire smoke.

A medium-sized dog of no discernable breed ran up as they approached. It barked enthusiastically and almost turned itself inside out with happy greetings.

David cupped the dog's face and gave it a rub.

"Ehvah, meet Sheila, and this is my Pop. Pop, this is Ehvah."

The man in front of David was as tall as him, but of slighter build. Despite his advanced age David's grandfather was a fit man. He wore a pair of long faded jeans, a flannel shirt, and a cowboy hat that was so decayed the frayed brim fell close to his eyebrows. His face was as weathered as the hat, but his light brown eyes were as bright and penetrating as David's.

He held out a thin hand. Ehvah was overpowered by a concrete shake. "Missy." His voice was as strong as his grip. "I hear you're in a bit of trouble—or you are a bit of trouble. One or the other."

Ehvah returned the firm handshake. David's advice to give as good as she got came to mind.

"That's funny. I hear the same about you." She accompanied the cheeky response with a smile planned to soften the slight.

Pop released her hand, and for a second she thought he looked a little taken aback. "Who'd you hear that from?"

She lifted one eyebrow and nodded towards David. "Who do you think?"

They both looked over at him. David lifted both hands high.

"What is this? You've known each other five seconds and you're already ganging up on me. Give a bloke a chance!"

Ehvah reached out and gave the top of his backpack a playful slap.

Sheila ran to her, barking in wild response to her mock assault on David.

Ehvah stopped short of flinching, and instead presented her hand for the dog to sniff.

"What kind of breed is she?" Ehvah couldn't pick any specific pedigree in Sheila's features.

"She's a bitsa,' Pop replied.

"Oh, I'm not familiar with that breed." Sheila gave her hand a nudge with her cold, wet nose.

Pop gave her a withering look. "It's not a breed, missy, it's a lota breeds. She's a bit Border collie, bit kelpie, bit cattle dog. She's a bitsa. Like a bita everything."

The Australian term made her laugh. "Well, that's something Sheila and I have in common."

Sheila turned a tight circle, barking in happy tone. She then pushed her snout into Ehvah's hand again.

"Humph. Well, you must be alright if the dog likes you. She's a good judge of character."

Ehvah gave Pop her best smile. Having Sheila's

approval clearly meant something to him.

Pop removed his hat and used it to gesture the way to the garage.

"Well, you pair might as well make yourselves at home. I got a stew on the stove and the billy's on the boil."

Ehvah decided not to ask what a billy was as she made her way to the unhinged door.

CHAPTER 27

"**W**here does this go?" Ehvah held up the serving spoon she had dried.

"In there." David indicated to an old set of drawers at the far end of the camp kitchen.

Ehvah deposited the spoon in the drawer. It held a bizarre mix of items, including firelighters and an assortment of nails. She picked up another wet utensil from the drying rack.

They had been here three days now, but she was still getting her bearings in the camp. It was a male environment. Nothing was ever in the obvious place. After cleaning the bathroom this morning, Ehvah had come to the conclusion that it could do with a woman's touch, but up until this moment she had been kept out of the kitchen.

Pop's lamb stew the first night had been a taste sensation. He explained he had been cooking it for hours over the open fire. A billy was a kettle that produced flavorsome tea.

The night they arrived, Pop had declared himself "chief cook and bottle washer", and everyone else was kept out of his kitchen. Ehvah didn't mind, as Pop was an excellent cook. Over the last three days she had discovered the culinary advantages of bush cooking. Depending on what he was preparing, Pop would throw a handful of leaves into the flames to season the smoke. They had just finished a meal of eucalypt-infused steak.

Although it wasn't served in a fancy restaurant, Ehvah had enjoyed every morsel. Her belly jutted out and rumbled with pleasure. She gave it a satisfactory pat.

"Was that you?" David's wide eyes and raised brows signified he had also heard her.

Ehvah giggled. "I think I ate too much. Everything was so delicious."

"Well, you certainly worked up an appetite today."

Ehvah took his comment as an immense compliment.

She had filled her days at the camp working on any task the men set her. She had weeded the garden, painted a door, emptied the rubbish, moved some rocks, and that afternoon she and Pop had dug up potatoes. Her usually manicured fingernails were so full of dirt that she had to cut them short. Even so, she had enjoyed every second with the older man, who was tough, but had an inner sweetness. As they worked together he encouraged her to share her life. They had even broken into song, as Pop pushed her to join him on numerous renditions of his old favorites. Ehvah enjoyed their heartfelt duet of *Amazing Grace*. Sheila had howled along with them.

The physical work had been a surprise pleasure. Ehvah lifted her arm and flexed.

"I think I may be getting some definition. What do you think?" She squeezed her fist as tight as she could to produce a bump in her upper arm.

David grinned in mock appreciation of her efforts.

"Like knots in cotton."

Ehvah flipped her towel at him before continuing to dry the dishes.

"It's been a long time since I did dishes." She rubbed another spoon.

"Leave them to air dry if you want. You've earned your keep today." David paused his chore to look sideways at her. His expression was kind and genuine, without a hint of condescension.

"No, I'm happy to do it. To be honest, it's nice to be useful."

She stopped to look out the open kitchen. Green foliage and a light blue sky filled her view. A navy channel patched with grey shadows from the afternoon clouds spread out in the distance, and a fresh breeze caught a faint whiff of ironbark smoke from the fire.

"I love that about this place. It's rough, but there's always so much purpose in every bit of the day." She didn't miss David's smile as he resumed washing the dishes.

"If you live in the bush, you have to get used to work. Nothing ever happens at the flip of a switch—you have to put some effort in."

"I've decided I like it. I like having a lot to do. The bush doesn't care who I am. It doesn't care that I have money. Like, today, I told a humongous spider not to come near me because I was a celebrity, and it took no notice of me."

She giggled at her earlier exchange with the arachnid. Pop had pointed it out to her, sitting inches from her leg. It was one thing to see the creatures in a book, but quite another to be face to face with one.

The huntsman was enormous, and it wasn't happy to be disturbed. Its body was the size of her big toe and the spindly legs jutted out at all angles. She had screamed and jumped out of the way. Pop had moved the creature with a stick and told her they were good to have around the camp because they ate the flying cockroaches in the summer. Ehvah had taken a horrified moment to wonder which was worse: a humongous spider running up her leg or a massive cockroach flying into her hair. After spending some time in the spider's company, she decided he was the lesser of the two evils.

"If you two are finished, put the billy on for a cuppa, will ya?" Pop called out from the garage adjacent to the kitchen.

David and Pop had explained that the garage structure was called a shed. Inside were two bedrooms, and an old, but now clean bathroom. David had moved in with Pop so she could have his room, which had the basic necessities: bed, cupboard and desk. The open-aired kitchen had a simple roof, and included an old iron stove and a refrigerator/freezer that ran off a solar-powered battery. The weather side of the kitchen was closed in, while the open side had wide eaves that stopped any rain from reaching the cooking space.

In the afternoons, the men lit what they called a donkey,

a steel barrel with a gas burner, to supply hot water. A pulley system from the base of the mountain provided an easier way of collecting supplies from the boat. It was rough but comfortable. The toilet flushed and the water was clean.

"You go and have a seat. I'll finish up here." David rubbed the aluminum bench with a rag.

"Come on, Sheila." Ehvah called to the dog who was lying on the floor of the kitchen.

The dog ambled behind her as they made their way down to chairs set up on a grassed area overlooking the channel.

David had explained that one side of the island had belonged to his uncle, but when he died, David had bought it off his cousins. The rest of the island had been sold to the National Parks. Pop acted as permanent caretaker.

Ehvah settled into a camp chair and marveled at how dramatically the sky had changed. Pastel streaks of pink and blue settled on the horizon, and the slight breeze that had floated through the trees at the back of the camp all day had now dropped to a dead calm. The channel and range spread out before her, waterways weaving through masses of green, and the range beyond blocked the setting sun.

A kookaburra landed on a tree close by, lifted his head and let out a loud, warbling cry.

Ehvah smiled. Its call did sound like it was laughing at her. The bird's head was cocked high as he shook his feathers. His mate landed next to him.

"I see you've met Bob and Mavis." David held out a steaming cup for her.

"Thank you." Ehvah reached up to take the tea from him. "You mean the kookaburras?"

David stood a guitar he was carrying up against his chair before taking a seat next to her and motioning up to the birds.

"Pop names the wildlife."

"Oh, that explains why I saw him talking to the trees yesterday."

Ehvah had giggled when she had seen Pop talking aloud to the branches. But the slight eccentricity was in keeping with his character, so she hadn't thought any more of the incident.

She looked up at the kookaburras. The blue wings on one bird were brighter than on the other.

"Are they different colors because one's male and the other's female?"

"They're a mating pair, but the plainer-looking one is a laughing kookaburra and the other's a blue-winged kookaburra. They don't often pair up, but I'd say they've lost their respective mates, found each other, and thought 'why not'?"

If birds can make it work, maybe there is hope for us.

A familiar feeling of longing washed over her, followed by a pang of despair.

Ehvah allowed a sigh to escape.

"That was a big one." David looked over before retrieving the guitar.

Why can't you see I've fallen in love with you and there's not a thing I can do about it?

She took a sip of her tea so she wouldn't voice her emotions. The sight of the setting sun over the unique tropical Australian view gave her an appreciation for where she was, even if there was no appreciation for their future together.

"This place is close to perfect."

David picked a tune on his guitar.

"You might not say that when the wind's blowing, or the rain's pelting down. This island's big and not far from the coast. The tropical climate means we get a lot of rain in the season."

He stopped working the strings to point to the back of the camp where the trees and scrub met the boundary.

"Just through there, about two hundred meters or so, is a big drop right down to the ocean. Most of the time we're protected and get the cool breeze, but sometimes it roars through there. It can also get humid when the wind doesn't blow. We've been lucky to have good weather."

"I wouldn't care if the wind blew and the rain pelted down, I'd still love it here. It's so raw and untouched. I feel inspired."

She picked up her journal.

David set about tuning the strings.

"Let's see if we can squeeze some more out of that inspiration. I've had something running around in my head all day." He picked out a tune before turning to her. "Would you read me that bit from this morning again?"

She scanned down to where she had been reading from her journal as they sat having coffee in the same spot earlier that day.

"My soul whips me with pain.

Remember the loss and relive shame.

Nowhere to go, nothing to hide, no memory unscathed, nothing is mine.

Then through fear you came and broke all the rules.

Chasing the night and bringing anew.

Now I look through different eyes.

Through grace, and love, and gift.

Hope is my friend,

My soul, you will lift,

Like a child to your arms and into your care.

Whatever is next I know, you'll be there."

David picked a few chords before shifting to a strum. He went through the riff several times before turning to her. "Have you got it?"

She nodded.

They worked together, with the tune he had developed, and the words she had written. Ehvah felt her voice soar louder and louder as she merged her poetry in harmony with his music. It felt so freeing to sing again, and to be singing the words she had written that morning felt like a dream. At times it was as though her voice belonged to someone else. Each word flowed off her breath, and the great joy she experienced when singing broke free, growing stronger and fusing in sync with the music David was playing.

When they finished he broke out into a broad smile. Ehvah knew her face mirrored his pleasure.

"That wasn't too bad." David picked over the strings as he spoke. "Again?"

They re-performed the short piece.

"How much have you written?"

Ehvah flipped through the pages of her journal. "A lot. Four pages in the last two days."

David's eyebrows rose. "This place is that inspiring?"

Ehvah reached down and grabbed the book at the side of her chair.

"Yeah, being here, but also this." She opened the Bible to the right spot. "I will never leave you nor forsake you."

She placed it in her lap on top of her open journal.

"I came across this bit underlined in red and it was like a penny dropped." She glanced down at the underlined words. They had truly inspired her. "I realized life isn't about understanding why God lets our loved ones leave us. It's about understanding that He will never leave us, no matter what. He doesn't always offer explanations as to why people die, but He does ask us to trust him when He says His love for us will never die."

She flipped to a bookmarked spot.

"I like this: 'If God is for us, who can be against us? For I am convinced that neither death nor life, neither angels nor demons, neither height nor depth, nor anything else in all of creation, will be able to separate us from the love of God that is in Christ Jesus our Lord'."

She looked up from her place.

"I realized nothing can ever separate us if we have faith, and trust in Him. It's not easy, but it's a promise He has made to us. And I know now that God's love for my parents went on, even after they died. His love for me went on, too. He's just been waiting for me to get that it's not about them and Him; it's about me and Him."

Tears welled and Ehvah sniffed as hard as she could to stop her nose from running. Her efforts produced a heavy snort through her nostrils. One look at David's surprised reaction to the ungainly noise sent them both into fits of laughter.

"Can I get you a tissue?"

She struggled to get her giggles under control. "No, thanks. I'm good."

She closed the Bible and fingered the cover. Pop had given it to her the day after she had arrived, and she had spent a lot of time reading it. The book looked as though it had once been bound in red leather, but the outside was worn. Inside the paper was a dingy yellow color. Underlined verses in various colored inks featured throughout.

"It was my grandmother's." David slid down a little in his chair.

"Really? When Pop gave it to me he said it was a spare."

"Pop's a pretty understated kind of bloke. He must like you. It's a real treasure." David's mouth tilted at the corners. "Gran used to say it was her most precious possession. She kept it by her bed so that if there was ever a fire and she had to get out quick she could grab it on the way."

The story made Ehvah smile. "When did she die?"

"About ten years ago. Pop's seventy-two this year. Not that he looks it."

"Wow, you're right. I would never have picked him to be that old."

A scuffing noise sounded behind them.

"Who's old?" Pop ambled up and stood next to David's chair. "You're not discussing your father's retirement?"

David shook his head. "Your son is your favorite topic, not mine."

Pop gave a decided "Humph. He's a pen pusher. Don't know why he's so tired of working. He's never done anything strenuous."

Ehvah heard David take a deep breath.

"My father's in logistics in the army, and he's just announced he's set to retire in two years. Pop's not impressed."

"Well, it's not like he's seen any action. Sitting at a desk all day moving things around. He may as well be playing Monopoly." Pop hurled the contents of his cupped hand out onto the grassed area beyond their seats.

The kookaburras swooped down to feed on the scraps of meat, thrashing the pieces of beef from side to side. Pop had explained they were trying to kill it the way they would a snake or lizard.

"I remember you saying your family had a history of military service."

Ehvah had treasured the snippet of personal information, and she would never forget the generational story behind the significance of his rising sun tattoo.

David stood to grab a dead branch from a pile of timber close by. He stuck it in the top of the silver bin on steel legs. It had served as the inner tub of a washing machine in its previous life, and was now a fireplace. The flames within cast enough warmth to keep them toasty in the cool evening air. Orange and yellow light flickered through the many holes in the side of the tub, making the new function of the object alluring.

"We've had a family member serve in just about every conflict in Australian history. Family have served in the Boer War and World War One. My great-grandfather served in World War Two. Pop served in Korea and Vietnam. My father has served in an administrative capacity. I've served in overseas offensives, and in peacekeeping operations."

"Ya never should've enlisted. I certainly didn't encourage you." Pop interrupted David's account.

"So you keep reminding me." David gave his grandfather a look from underneath low brows.

Pop pushed the protruding stick further into the steel pot fire.

"I told 'im to forget the army and keep at his music. That's what he loved. He was good at it, too. Your father was pushing ya to join up. He had this big idea that there was nothing for you but the army. You can't live your life through ya kids."

Pop looked over to Ehvah.

"What'd you say, missy? You've got a music background. Is he any good or what?"

Ehvah wondered if the pink color shading David's face was embarrassment over his grandfather's comments or reflections from the last light of the day. It was satisfying to think he might be rattled for a change.

"He's a great musician, and a better guitarist than a lot

of professionals I've played with."

Her first morning at the camp she had found David at this spot picking on his guitar. He had explained that he kept one up at the camp so he could play when he visited. It was obvious that he played from the heart, and that was a rare and valuable thing.

"Well, you two sounded pretty good just then. Maybe you should do something together." Pop stood up tall, visibly proud of his grandson.

David gave his grandfather a lopsided smile. "Righto, Pop." He turned to her. "I guess we could give it a go. Do you want to work some more on this song?"

Ehvah couldn't contain the flurry of excitement in her heart. "I'd love that."

***

Mara sat in the rental car and watched Lyle's body language as he talked. He swayed towards the elderly woman and dropped one shoulder to lean into her. The woman remained stock still and shook her head in deliberate resolve.

"What is he doing?"

Vinnie bent to one side of the vehicle's back seat and watched out of the window. "Turning on the charm, like he always does."

Mara could see that Lyle's suave ploy wasn't working on his target. The grey-haired lady in the flowery print dress set her shoulders, widened her stance, and gripped the handle of her walking stick.

Mara struck the middle of the steering wheel, setting off the car horn. He was wasting time. This lady wasn't going to give them the information they needed.

Both the lady and Lyle looked their way. The elderly woman frowned and pursed her wrinkled lips. Lyle dropped his jaw and tilted his head.

"Argh. Why can't he see this is futile?" Mara rolled her eyes.

Lyle focused back on the lady, who was still giving Mara a cold hard stare. He said something, then reached out to touch the hem of the lady's sleeve.

The woman wielded her walking stick high and pounded it down over Lyle's shoulder with one fell swoop. Lyle flinched, covering his head with his arms while the lady unleashed a torrent of abuse on him.

Mara couldn't hear what she was saying, but the woman's unappreciative tone carried on the ocean breeze. The woman waved her stick, poised for another blow as Lyle bolted back to the car, ducking all the way.

He leaped into the front next to Mara.

"Did you see that? The natives are not friendly." He smoothed his hair back into place.

The elderly lady shook her fist, then continued on her way down the street.

Mara rolled her eyes and started the car.

"This has to be the right place. We need to find someone who can tell us where the security man lives."

They drove back through the houses, and onto the main road out of town.

"Go down there."

Vinnie reached over the center console from the back seat and pointed to a dirt track that veered to the left. Mara pulled a sharp turn and travelled the length of the narrow trail through the swampy landscape.

"I thought the rainforest was bad, but this place is the pits." Lyle adjusted the air-conditioning vent to blow on him.

"There." Vinnie pointed again to a break in the trees. "Stop the car."

Mara pulled off the dirt track. Vinnie exited the back seat.

Mara could see him picking his way through the high grass until he reached a makeshift shack. The construction consisted of pieces of tin secured to a tree. An old man came out of the structure.

Vinnie lit a cigarette and offered it to the man, who had the classic look of a homeless vagabond. He then reached into his pocket and gave the man a handful of Australian notes. Mara couldn't make out how much, only that the notes were yellow—fifty dollar notes.

Vinnie slapped the man on the back and sauntered back to the car. He settled into his seat.

"Head back to the main road. I know where they are."

CHAPTER 28

Ehvah borrowed David's cell and took up position outside the camp kitchen. Reception was better in the open.

"Agent Gregson?"

"Ehvah. I'm calling to give you a quick update. We are making progress, but we have yet to find the location of the deposit."

Ehvah let go of the breath she had been holding.

"The personal items you gave us were clean."

She bit her lip. A mixture of frustration and relief flooded her. Frustration that she was still in danger, and relief that she wasn't going to be separating from David anytime soon.

"I want you to stay where you are until you hear from me. Can you do that?"

"Yes."

"And, Ehvah, call me immediately if your aunt manages to contact you. We don't have anything concrete on her, but I have a hunch she's involved in this somehow."

Ehvah nodded, even though Gregson couldn't see her. "Not a problem. I share your hunch."

They exchanged goodbyes and she disconnected the call.

"What news?" Pop called out from the kitchen.

Ehvah moved back to them and relayed the details of the conversation.

"Well, looks like you're stuck with us for a bit longer, missy." Pop wrapped an arm around her shoulders and gave her a cuddle.

Ehvah smiled up at him.

David began the task of collecting the breakfast dishes.

"Why don't you set up down there and I'll be along in a few minutes." He tilted his chin towards their favorite place on the grassy area.

Pop gave her a pat on the back and she wandered down to the spot. She and David had spent a lot of time sitting here in previous days. They worked on their song, talked, or relaxed after a hard day's work around the camp.

"Hello there, you two," she called to Bob and Mavis high in the trees above the lookout.

They lifted their heads and let out a laughing cry.

At times it seemed like unnatural torture to be there, knowing it was unlikely she and David would share a future together. Now that Gregson had confirmed a longer stay, Ehvah promised herself to enjoy their time while it lasted. She had worked hard to curb her physical reactions to him, and she suspected he had done the same.

She picked up the book on her chair and took a seat. They had begun to sit down after breakfast each day and read a Bible verse together. Sometimes it was one from her Bible that David's grandmother had highlighted, other times it was one David wanted to share with her.

"Ready?" David took a seat beside her, Bible in hand.

She sat up straight.

"I've got a good one for today. It's from John." She opened to the specified spot. She had come across a section David's grandmother had highlighted with a pink pencil. A small flower drawing had been created in the margin. The words 'Even when it doesn't make sense', were written in pink next to the verse.

Ehvah checked to see if David was ready before reading.

"There is no fear in love. But perfect love drives out fear, because fear has to do with punishment. The one who fears is not made perfect in love. We love because He first loved us."

Interesting. Fear had been a driving force in her life since the death of her family. First, fear that she would feel their loss too greatly drove her to work hard. Then fear that she would be alone inspired her to stay connected with people who didn't love her. Fear that there was nothing left for her in the entertainment industry drove her to give up, and live a party lifestyle, and fear for her life drove her to withhold information about James's death.

God says perfect love drives out fear. He showed us how to love without fear.

Ehvah closed her eyes.

Please help me not to fear to love, Lord. Even when it doesn't make sense.

She opened her eyes and looked up at David. His deep brown eyes held magnetic intensity and Ehvah felt her pulse quicken to a screaming pace. How could she hold to her vow to keep herself in check when he looked at her this way?

Just kiss me, touch me, hold my hand . . . something.

Her eyes must have conveyed her longing because he reached over and took her hand. His touch sent a river of warmth flowing up her arm and into her body. His dark chocolate eyes danced a depth of emotion. She was certain that he was fighting an attraction to her. The inspiration of the reading joined with his touch and gave her hope that they could work out their differences.

His thumb stroked the inside of her palm sparking a tingling in her body that made the modest gesture feel like extraordinary seduction.

A fit of barking broke through their moment. Sheila was standing some distance off. She bounced up and down in vibrant alert.

"Stay here."

David dropped her hand and walked towards the dog. At first Ehvah thought the large log stretching over the grass next to Sheila was a fallen branch, but as the trunk inched with movement it became evident that it was an enormous snake.

The revelation made her jump to her feet and stagger back a few meters.

"David, it's a snake!" she screamed over the dog's growling.

David looked back from his position next to Sheila. He had one hand on the dog, who retreated at the command.

"It's okay. Don't panic. Stay right there."

Ehvah could feel her eyes wide in their sockets. Every pulse point in her body hammered. She froze in stunned horror as David prompted Sheila to sit.

David walked back to her. Sheila sat obediently next to the snake. He took her hand and held it firm. Ehvah could feel her arm shake beyond his grip. His eyes linked with hers.

"Don't panic. It's a carpet python. They aren't venomous, and it won't hurt you. His name's Bernie and he lives in the camp."

Ehvah knew her mouth had dropped open, but didn't possess sufficient motor skills to close it. She took a second to process what he had said. This creature lived in the camp?

"I've been living with a snake and you didn't tell me?" Her voice was high and squeaky.

"I didn't tell you because I knew you would stress, and we don't see him often. He usually stays hidden around the shed."

"What?"

Her eyes darted from the snake to David and back again.

"Ehvah." David had placed one hand under her chin and guided her gawk from the snake to connect back with him. His eyes locked with hers.

"I know snakes are symbols of evil, but they're also animals. Like all animals Bernie's got a temperament, and he's actually tame. We wouldn't let him hang around if he was a threat. He'll even let us pick him up and move him if he's in the way." He gave her hands a gentle squeeze.

"He probably came out of hiding to say hello to you." Ehvah sucked in her breath.

David's mouth twitched, then broke into a smile.

"I'm not asking you to go anywhere near him, but now he's here, it's a good opportunity for you to see the difference between the evil symbol and the animal."

A ball of horror was stuck in her throat. She'd been living with a snake. The words she had read moments before stuck in her mind. *Perfect love drives out fear.*

Lord, I don't know that I will ever love Bernie the snake. But I can at least try to understand him.

She took a deep breath and nodded.

David dropped one of her hands and stood beside her.

"Just stay here with me and watch him. I don't like snakes either, and to be honest, I wish Bernie would find somewhere else to live. But just like kookaburras and the huntsman spiders, he plays an important role here."

Ehvah could see the chinks and contours of Bernie's scaly skin.

"We used to have a problem with rats until Bernie took up residence. For the most part, Bernie also keeps the dangerous snakes away. He's pretty cool. Watch how his body moves."

As they watched the creature, Ehvah came to appreciate his grace. His long body slinked inch by inch as it progressed through the undergrowth. The motley olive pattern on Bernie's skin was decorated with spots of brown and black. He was shiny and fluid.

As several minutes passed, her throbbing heart returned to a moderate pace.

David kept hold of her hand as the tip of Bernie's tail disappeared under a bush.

"Are you good?"

Ehvah nodded. "Just don't expect me to touch it."

David laughed. "That's fine."

Even though she had survived her introduction to Bernie, the thought of him sent a cold shiver up her spine.

Any close contact with that creature was unacceptable. She decided that while she could appreciate his reptilian beauty and movement, she had no desire to befriend him. The fact that he hung around the shed rafters in plain sight was enough for her to decide to never, ever look up. Where Bernie was concerned, out of sight, out of mind was the way to go.

CHAPTER 29

Ehvah swam up to the edge of the water hole and pulled her body erect to hang off the smooth rock ledge. Below her was another larger pool, and beyond that a waterfall cascaded down the mountain, dropping into a creek that flowed fresh water out to sea.

The view on this side of the island was just as spectacular as the camp view. The ocean stretched out before her, with blue, green and grey patterns merging together as far as her eye could see. A group of islands broke the vast blue on the right of the horizon. They were a long way off, but still visible in the freshness of the clear day.

It was a twenty-minute walk from the camp to the waterfall. The path wound up a steep rocky formation and through a dense piece of bush, but the trek was worth it. David had introduced her to the area two days ago. Even though the water was cold, she had begged him to bring her back to the pristine spot to swim, enjoy the view, and see to some of the hygienic necessities she found hard to do in the camp, like washing her hair.

The camp ran on rain water, harvested through guttering and collected in several tanks. Pop had told her that they rarely ran out of fresh water, but as they were in the dry season, water conservation was vital.

Over the last week, Ehvah had resisted washing her hair and had worn some clothing twice. It had been a relief to hand wash her garments in the crystal clear waters. While she washed, she prayed.

She was starting to get better at praying. Not that it was a skill to master, but sharing her thoughts and fears with God was getting easier. Now when she closed her eyes it felt as though a presence was next to her—or coming through her, she wasn't sure which—but whenever she prayed or thought about God, this presence was there.

The feeling reminded her of one of her parent's songs, *Flowing Spirit.* It was part of the collection they had never recorded. The lyrics talked about God's Spirit and how it was like the wind. You never knew where it had come from, or where it was going, but you knew it existed by its presence.

Apart from praying about the situation with the crime mob, Ehvah had also started praying for her aunt. It wasn't easy, and sometimes her mouth would be asking God to help Mara, while inside she harbored a seething bitterness for the lack of love her aunt had shown her. Even so, she persevered in the hope that one day her feelings would match the blessing she asked for.

The sudden call of a butcherbird high in the water hole's bordering gum trees broke through her thoughts. In the week she had been at the camp she had come to recognize some of the native birds and animals. She smiled as she watched the nimble black and white bird swoop down over the water, then dip in with a sudden splash, emerging seconds later.

The bird's quick dip reminded her that the cool mountain water was a lot colder while she remained still. She took one last look at the view, then swam back to the shallow rocks.

She scanned the area to ensure there were no hazardous creatures in her vicinity before exiting the water. She had avoided another encounter with Bernie, and preferred to remain unaware of any other crawling or creeping things.

Although Bernie was a reminder of James's murderer, Ehvah was surprised to find the appearance of the creature hadn't escalated the severity of her nightmares. In fact, she hadn't had one nightmare since arriving at the camp. It seemed her renewed faith had a lot to do with her peace of mind.

She fingered a pair of jeans and cotton t-shirt as they flopped on a low lying branch. It was a split-second decision to wash the clothes she had worn to the water hole. The drip-drying process was taking a lot longer than she anticipated.

Accompanying them were another two sets of clothing she had brought to wash. The only dry thing she had was a towel.

The thought of having two extra sets of clean clothes had been too attractive a prospect to pass up. She reasoned that even if she had to wear a damp set home, it would be worth it. She hadn't realized dripping wet clothes took so much longer to dry than the machine-spun version. All her clothes were so wet that putting them back on to wear in the cool breeze would be torture.

Ehvah decided that the best option was to get out of the water, wrap herself in her towel and sit in the sun in the hope that they dried off fast.

That's what I get for never doing my own laundry.

She wrung out the bra she had been swimming in to add it to the stack of drying garments, and kept her knickers on while she wrapped herself up.

David had let her stay at the waterhole on her own, knowing she needed some privacy. The first time they had visited he had taken a dip then spent some time fishing. This time he had checked out the area, then left her to enjoy the water. He had assured her he would be close by, a little way down the walking track in case any backpackers or national park rangers ventured to the waterhole while she was there. She was supposed to meet him back on the track over ten minutes ago.

He's going to come looking for me.

Ehvah glanced down the track for signs of life. That would be great; David turning up while she was dressed in nothing but a towel!

She considered using her coo-ee call, but stupidity didn't constitute an emergency. Within minutes, a head of brown hair rounded the corner. Ehvah felt her stomach drop.

Oh, no.

"What are you doing? I was starting to get worried." David's head cocked to one side and his mouth twisted as he stood watching her.

"I washed all my clothes and they're still soaking."

Her ridiculous confession was met with a roaring chuckle.

"Why did you wash all your clothes?"

She tightened the towel under her armpits.

"They were all dirty and I thought at least one set would dry in a few minutes." She stopped to give him her best sheepish look. "I don't do a lot of laundry. At home, everything goes in the dryer."

David dropped his backpack on the ground. He shook his head and set about removing his t-shirt.

"Here, this'll cover you. Wrap the towel around your waist."

His grin stretched across his face as he handed her the shirt.

Ehvah felt her face burn, though she didn't know if it was from her own embarrassment or from the fact that they were both only semi-clothed.

David turned his back in an effort to protect her modesty as she pulled the shirt over her head. It smelt like his deodorant, spicy and warm. She stopped to breathe in the scent, then loosened the towel to secure it around her waist. As she tucked in the edge of the fabric she felt a strange slimy patch under her left ribcage.

Ehvah tried to twist in an effort to see what it was. All she could make out was that it was something black.

"Argh." Her warbling cry echoed over the water hole. "There's something on me."

"What?"

"There's a black thing on me." She tried to pull at it, but whatever it was wouldn't budge. "It won't come off. Get it off. Get it off."

She jumped up and down in a frantic attempt to dislodge it.

David whipped around, and for a second she forgot about the creature and checked to ensure the towel was covering her.

He traveled the few feet between them.

"Stop panicking. Where it is?"

Ehvah pulled the shirt up under her breasts and lifted as high as she could to reveal the area on her left ribcage.

"What it is?"

David squatted down to see.

"It's a leech."

"Ugh." A surge of revulsion make her insides lurch. "How did I get a leech on me? Is it sucking my blood? Is it poisonous?"

He reached into his pocket.

"You would have picked it up from the mud in the shallows. Yes, it is sucking your blood. No, it's not poisonous." The look on his face was pure amusement.

"Why would you think this is funny? Maybe we should just leave it there and take it back to the camp so Pop can name it."

David pulled open a box of matches. His smile broadened at her sarcastic comment.

"What are you going to do with that?" What did fire have to do with her predicament?

David prepared to light a match.

"I'm getting the leech off. Unless you prefer to leave it there and wait until it drops off?"

Ehvah could feel the horror on her face.

"They drop off?"

"When they get their fill of your blood."

"Eww. Do it."

"I'm going to blow this out and hold the hot end to the leech's backside. It'll drop right off." He poised in position and struck a match. "Hold still, otherwise I might burn you."

Ehvah closed her eyes tight, steeling herself for the procedure.

"So that's your tattoo?"

She looked down to see David staring at a spot just above the leech. The t-shirt was high enough to uncover the ink, but low enough to screen her chest. He cocked his head to one side and frowned at the spot.

Ehvah stamped her foot. There was no time for this. "Can we get this done please?"

"I've been wondering where it was."

The knowledge that he had been contemplating her body art inspired a pang of delight. Then she remembered that his procrastination was allowing a bloodsucker to hang off her.

"Can we discuss this later? One day it's giant spiders, then giant snakes, now I've got a giant leech attached to my body, sucking my blood and giving me goodness knows what diseases." Yes, the diva-like outburst was over-the-top, but surely he could understand the gravity of the situation.

He grimaced as he flipped the match to the ground. It had burned down to the end. David stared at her. His eyebrows lowered.

"That's a bit dramatic. I just wanted to know what your tattoo was about. You know all about mine." His lips pursed and forehead wrinkled into a deep frown.

Ehvah felt her patience disappear. She was in dire need of medical treatment.

"It's not like I kept it from you. I'm happy to share the significance, but the topic hasn't come up. Besides, it's not like you get close enough to me to find it." She paused to let out a heavy huff before continuing. "I'm some sort of untouchable to you. It's like I'm completely repulsive. And now I've got a bloodsucker attached to me and I'm genuinely repulsive."

The instant it was out of her mouth she regretted the aimless rant. All the pent-up emotion, the intensity of her attraction for him, and the seeming hopeless nature of their future all burst out before she had a chance to think.

David's frown deepened and his dark eyes connected with hers making her squirm.

"Is that what you think? That I'm repulsed by you?"

Ehvah licked her dry lips. Exasperation set in. She knew he wasn't repulsed, but he was driving her crazy.

"I don't know, David."

He sighed, so deep and heavy that Ehvah saw his bare chest rise and fall with the effort. A queasy feeling circulated her abdomen. Focusing on his pectoral muscles was a bad idea.

"I'm sorry I've made you feel like that. It's hard for me to allow myself to get close to people."

Ehvah focused on the rocks at her feet. "Well, that's not so easy for me either."

David rubbed the back of his neck. "It's not just that. I keep myself in check because I can't think to protect you when all I think about is . . ."

He held one palm up while the other remained behind his head. He wouldn't look at her.

A sense of frustration rose within her.

He's never going to make a move.

The thought sprung her into action. She let the t-shirt drop and closed the distance between them. In one swift movement, she wrapped her arms around his neck, reached up on tip toe and pulled her body to his.

The second their lips met it felt as though every bit of torturous tension between them melted away.

Ehvah kissed him with abandon, forcing every trace of resolve to vanish.

His lips were soft at first but seconds into the kiss, they hardened. His arms encircled her waist, pulling her hips towards his. His hands created warm patches in the small of her back.

The kiss went on as it phased through different crescendos, him taking control and loving her the way she needed, then pulling away, and reconnecting with her again.

When they parted it felt like as though they had ridden a violent roller coaster. They both stood rooted to the spot for a moment before she came to a horrible realization.

"I still have a leech attached to me."

CHAPTER 30

David shifted to see beyond the shed wall so he could check on Ehvah's position. She hadn't moved from the picnic blanket on the grassed area, and was deep in concentration, practicing guitar chords.

They had made it back from the waterhole in record time. David was still in shock over what had happened, and the way he had lost control.

After they had parted, he had seen to the leech situation, and had bolted back to the camp. Ehvah had maintained the pace he set, which was breakneck. They hadn't spoken. She had set up a blanket on the grass, and he had busied himself chopping wood. The hard physical work had helped alleviate his pent up emotions— disappointment at his abandonment, disgust at his lack of professionalism, and admittance that he loved her so much it was killing him when it wasn't driving him crazy. Either way, it wasn't good.

He could hear Pop turning the sausages on the fire behind him. Each one burst with a fierce sizzle as the uncooked side met the grill.

"What are you waiting for?" Pop's asked over the splattering.

David faced his grandfather. "What do you mean?"

"Her." Pop motioned to Ehvah with his set of cooking tongs. "If you don't show some interest soon, you'll miss out. Have a go, boy."

David felt the corners of his mouth tilt up. If only his grandfather knew what had transpired that afternoon. He was still amazed that she had taken the lead, something that he wasn't accustomed to in a relationship. He was always the one in control, the driving force, making the moves. Yet it had been the most amazing feeling to hold her in his arms and kiss her. At times he felt as though he was free to love her, then a little voice would creep in telling him what a bad idea it was. Instinct repeated over and over that any relationship he had with Ehvah was fraught with danger, and danger was something he had left behind years ago.

"It's not as simple as having a go. There's a lot to consider."

"No, there's not. Who cares that you're both from different places? You have enough in common. She's good for you."

"Is that right?"

Pop stopped flipping to give him a direct look.

"Too right, lad. She's got a fire in her belly. She's not scared to stick it to you and tell you how it is. That's the sign of a good woman. One who challenges you to be a better man is one worth keeping."

"It's not about the challenge." David watched Ehvah. Her blonde hair fell onto her shoulders as her head tilted towards the guitar on her lap. "I don't know if I can go through the drama. She's a star from Hollywood. It's pretty full on."

Pop burst into roaring laughter—not the reaction he was expecting.

"Boy, where there's women, there's always drama. Haven't you worked that out yet? Doesn't matter one bit if they're a movie star or a regular gal. Besides, it's got nothing to do with drama. You're scared."

David shook his head at the old man's presumption.

"How do you figure that?" He forced a heavy expulsion of air from his nostrils in an effort to drive home his indignation.

"You're a soldier. You know how to go into battle, fight, keep your cool under pressure, but the thought of having a serious relationship leaves you shaking in your boots."

Pop set about flipping the sausages again.

David formed his best withering look. "How did you

come up with this theory, Professor?"

"It's no theory. Its history repeating itself. We Blake men all know how to fight. What we don't know how to do is love. It's something we have to learn the hard way."

David's face must have reflected his confusion because Pop went on.

"My parents never got on. Dad was a tough bloke, but he had no idea about relationships. Your father's the same. Maybe if he'd seen some action, he'd understand that he doesn't have all the answers and that he needs God." Pop raised bushy, grey eyebrows as he spoke.

"I used to be like that too, but my time in the army affected me like it did you. I was all about being tough and sticking it out. What I didn't work out, until much later, was that real toughness is to give it over to God and get help. Admitting you don't have all the answers and taking a chance—that's tough, it's smart, and it's faith at work. God responds to that."

"What made you realize this?" David couldn't recall Pop ever talking extensively about his time straight out of the army.

Pop stopped to give some attention to the sausages before answering.

"I was blessed. I had your grandmother. She was a quiet soul, but she didn't give up on me. Not once. And she never stopped challenging me, either. She prayed for me and stuck by me even when everyone told her to give up. By all accounts, she should have."

David recalled the margin note Ehvah had read him out of his grandmother's Bible, 'Even when it doesn't make sense'. "I remember her telling me that when it comes to marriage, faith and perseverance go hand in hand. She must have had faith that things would work out?"

Pop nodded. "Your grandmother had faith in God, not in me, mind you, but in His ability to heal me. And He did. Not right away, but slowly, and only after I gave in to His way, yet she stuck it out. She trusted that God has us together for His purpose."

Pop pointed the tongs at him.

"You need to get past worrying about how this relationship will go. God's put you and that girl together for His reasons. You need to trust in His plan and stop trying to make sense of it or work it out to suit your reasoning. It's not going to be easy, but no relationship ever is."

Pop looked out to Ehvah. "I can tell you this much, lad. God's in it, and He's much bigger than Hollywood. It'll be right."

"I hear what you're saying but I just don't see how it's going to work." David let out a heavy sigh.

Pop waved the tongs high in the smoky air. "Boy, it's not for you to see - it's for you to trust. To everything there is a season. God's kept you to Himself so He could heal you. You've trusted Him through that, so now it's time to trust Him through this new season."

David felt like a great weight had been dropped on him. Hearing his own wisdom about seasons come back on him was something he didn't anticipate.

Pop didn't seem to notice his turmoil. "God's given you both an honest love for each other. Blind Freddy can see that! Quite frankly, it's making me mad the way you two look at each other but won't do anything about it."

Pop was right. He wasn't just holding back because that was the easier way to protect her. He was holding back because it was the easy way to protect himself.

Time to trust in you, Lord.

The weight lifted.

***

Ehvah closed her eyes and concentrated on the tune. The song she and David had written was finished, so now they had to perfect the timing. As she widened her throat to hit the higher notes, she marveled at how beautifully her lyrics meshed with David's music. Never before had she felt so connected to a song.

Her previous recordings were all aimed at the teenage market, written by songwriters who churned out commercial hits for the network's stars. The songs were never aimed at showcasing her voice or complementing her personal tastes.

The aim had been to make the money for the network, and give the target audience what they wanted. This song was about her and David, their lives, and their faith in God. It was raw and personal, and Ehvah felt a sense of power flow through her as she sang.

Concentrating on the song had been a good distraction from the morning's events. David was avoiding her, and she didn't blame him. As good as it felt to be in his arms and have his lips on hers, it was wrong of her to force him into that position. Her insides constricted with regret when she recalled the way he had bolted back to the camp. Had she made it impossible for them to still be friends?

She placed the guitar flat on her lap and took a moment to appreciate the view.

We could never have been just friends. It wouldn't have been enough.

The thought simulated hot tears behind her eyes. The rustling sound of someone approaching made her swallow hard. David took a seat beside her on the picnic rug before she had a chance to compose herself and look up.

"You have an amazing voice."

Heat travelled to her cheeks. "Thanks, but I think a lot of it has to do with the song. I don't remember ever sounding this good." The nervous energy inside produced a giggle.

Great. Now instead of a femme fatale, I sound like some sort of pathetic schoolgirl with a crush.

He was sitting so close she could breathe in his scent. It was a heady mixture of spicy aftershave and iron bark smoke from the campfire. Ehvah felt her stomach sink as she recalled what his lips felt like on hers. The memory plunged her further into a confused and nervous state.

Push it down, at least he's talking to you now.

She racked her brain for a safe topic.

"A producer once told me that I sounded like Karen Carpenter, but then a different one told me I sounded more like my father than my mother. I don't know how I can possibly sound male. That was weird . . . I don't know."

OK. Stop talking. Just stop talking.

If she could have rolled her eyes without his noticing

she would have. She sounded tongue-tied and pathetic.

David crossed his long legs at the ankle and leaned back on his hands.

"I can see some similarities to Karen Carpenter. Didn't they say her voice was like honey, or something like that? You have that trait. It's deep, but it's clear. It's unique. To be honest, I've never heard any of your other singles, so I can't compare this song to anything you've done in the past."

Now she did allow her eyes to roll.

"You didn't miss much. They made me sing an octave higher than what comes naturally and I hated it. It came out fake and forced. The teen audience at the time didn't seem to mind. They downloaded the singles and made the network happy. For a few years, anyway. I'd rather not sing at all than sing like that again."

"Well, your passion for this song shines through."

Just like my passion for you.

Ehvah fiddled with the strings, then handed him the guitar.

"Should we give it a run though?" If she was singing, she wasn't saying something stupid.

David took the instrument and played the opening notes of the song. He was a talented guitarist. It was a pleasure to watch his fingers move along the strings. Ehvah had an instant reminder of how those hands felt caressing her back a few hours earlier. Her body's response to the memory almost threw her off the opening mark.

The song progressed without a hitch. Ehvah kept her eyes closed to the last note. Each time the song finished she wished it wasn't the end. She gave a deep sigh as she thought about her time with David coming to an end.

It's not fair, Lord. Why can't he see that we're good together? With you on our side, we can make it work. I know we can.

Ehvah felt movement next to her and she opened her eyes to find David's face inches away.

Without saying a word, his lips met hers. As her heart rate soared, the passion she felt for him released, and there was no doubt that he responded in kind. That morning she had known he was at odds with his emotions. This time there was no hesitation. His need engulfed her, taking her over. Ehvah fell into blissful submission.

His hand slipped around her waist, pulling her to him as his fingers massaged her side. She returned his touch, resting one hand on his chest and feeling the contours of his torso.

As they parted his head tilted to run a string of tiny kisses down the side of her neck. The sensation produced a tingle that ran up her spine, and she shivered with pleasure. She tilted her head further as he reached her collarbone.

Ehvah closed her eyes as his fingers moved further up her side, then stopped. She waited for him to continue, but he didn't.

"Someone's watching us."

Ehvah opened her eyes to find Sheila sitting on the edge of the blanket, wagging her tail. Her big brown eyes were fixed on them. She let out an ear-piercing yelp, then raced up to the shed.

The interruption made them both laugh.

"Sheila hasn't seen anyone kissing before. I think she was making sure we were both okay."

Ehvah moved her hand to encircle David's neck. "It's nice to know she cares."

David focused back on her. His eyes filled with raw emotion, and Ehvah felt her spirit soar with hope. He looked down at his hand. His fingers moved just under her ribcage where the leech had attached, and he had seen her tattoo.

They hadn't discussed the inking. Ehvah could see he wanted to ask her about the tiny line of red numbers and letters that sat hidden under her left breast.

"It's the co-ordinates of a little coastal town we would all sneak away to when Mom and Dad were alive. Nobody knew about it, but it's where most of their number one hits were written. It's close to where their plane went down."

He dropped his hand from the spot.

"The co-ordinates are followed by their birth dates and initials. I had it done years ago, on the seventh anniversary of their death. Seven was my Mom's lucky number, so it seemed appropriate." She shrugged.

"Nice." David smiled.

"I wanted a reminder of them close to my heart. I don't talk about it, and nobody ever sees it because of where it is. James was one of the few people who knew about it. He came across the receipt for the artist years go."

She was thankful now that she had shared the intimate story with her uncle. The secret of her tattoo was a connection between them. Now that he was gone it was comforting to know they had once had that connection.

"No one sees it. Well, unless a leech attaches itself to the spot and I have to lift my shirt up so a man can poke a hot stick on its butt to make it fall off."

She smiled and felt heat mark her cheeks at the memory.

So embarrassing.

David's grin spread over his face.

"That's a beautiful tribute to them. See, not all tattoos are symbols of violence."

Ehvah smiled back at him.

"You must miss being with your parents. Was the little town anything like the ones here?" David reached out to caress her side.

"It was in Mexico, so it was different culture, but I think one of the reasons I felt so at peace at the beach house— and now here—is because of the connection with my childhood. It's a shame about the horrible circumstances that brought me here, but I'm glad I came."

"All we need for you to be free is a call from the FBI to say they've found the location of the money. James hid it well if they're still looking for it." David lifted his eyebrows.

"I can't believe they haven't found it by now. They have everything I own. James must have put it somewhere unexpected if they're still searching." Ehvah pinched lint balls from the mat.

"Where is this place you visited with your parents?" His eyebrows furrowed.

"Just over the border in Mexico. Why?"

"Was it a built-up area? Did the town have shops and

houses, or was it more of a village?"

"It was just a village, but there were larger shops close by. The greengrocer sent me a beautiful letter saying how much he would miss my parents. He encouraged me to go back and visit them all, but I never could. It was too painful."

Maybe it's time to go back.

"You said James knew about it because of your tattoo."

"That's right. He was one person who had the full story. I know he never told Mara about it, because she would have had something smart to say for sure."

"Was there a bank in the village?"

She took a moment to think. Sudden realization set in. She knew where he was going.

"Yes. There is a bank. Are you thinking . . .?"

"Did your uncle make any reference to your tattoo or the town before he died?"

It took a second to think of a time when James would have been reminded of her tattoo.

She explained the week prior to the shooting when her stiletto heel had broken and James had helped her up off the floor. His grumpy reference to her tattoo had sparked an argument between them.

"That's it, then. I reckon there's a good chance the money's sitting in a bank in Mexico."

Ehvah's smile was broad. "The theory's so crazy, I think you might be right."

"We need to get hold of that agent." David moved the guitar and came to stand.

Ehvah sighed. It looked as though the mystery could be solved, but what did that mean for their relationship?

CHAPTER 31

Mara swallowed hard to stop the sick feeling in her stomach erupting.

"How much longer?"

The skipper of the charter boat looked back from his place at the wheel.

"About half an hour. This is the worst bit."

She grabbed her hand bag and staggered to the back of the boat where Lyle and Vinnie were taking turns being sick over the side.

"Will you two get a grip? Surely there's nothing left inside you now. All your hurling is starting to make me feel ill."

"I've never been so sick in all my life," Lyle groaned from his position on an upturned bucket. His face had an unmistakable green tinge.

Vinnie rested his elbows on the edge of the boat, head in his hands. He glanced their way. "Me either."

Mara bent down to their level so the skipper wouldn't hear. "Ehvah had better be there, or I'm going to kill you both."

Vinnie stared at her, his eyes flashing a restrained rage that made her pull back.

"Well, it's the only lead we've got." Lyle rubbed his forehead.

Mara scoffed. "Your lead comes from a drunk living in a shack in a swamp. He could have told you anything."

Vinnie picked up the bottom of his blue shirt and wiped his mouth with the hem, prompting her to gag. "Drunks are one source you can trust. They've got nothing to lose by telling the truth.”

Mara tried to pat the creases out of her tailored pants. “For all our sakes, I hope you’re right.”

***

David strained to reach the connection on the base of the antenna. One touch confirmed the cable was loose. He gave it a firm push and retrieved his cell phone from his pocket. Full service had resumed.

He had tried to call Agent Gregson several times since he and Ehvah had discovered the possible connection between her tattoo and the missing money. But the cell phone signal was weak, and he’d only managed to get part of the story out before the connection was cut off. Now he’d fixed the antenna, he could call Gregson back. Hopefully this was the information she needed to move forward and see Ehvah out of danger. If all parties to this crime knew the FBI had secured the money, they would have no reason to pursue her.

David checked the cord once more before moving to the ladder. He could make the call from the ground. Sheila’s frantic barking forced him to pause and look over the edge of the roof. The dog was outside the shed door, growling.

Pop appeared next to her.

“That’s it. I’m gonna tie you up. You’ve been going off at him all day, and he’s just doing his job. If you keep jumping up at him, you’re gonna hurt yourself.” Pop looked up to the outside wall of the shed. “You go about your business, Bernie.”

He pulled Sheila over to the far corner next to her bed, then attached the lead to her collar.

“The day you catch the rats is the day I’ll get rid of the snake. You got it?” His tone may have been gruff but he gave Sheila an affectionate rub behind the ears.

David checked Ehvah’s position on the blanket to ensure she wasn’t aware that Bernie was on the move. He didn’t want her to stress.

He could see her pushing Pop’s reading glasses back against her face as she scanned her journal. Gregson had taken her prescription pair. She was oblivious to Bernie's presence.

He gathered his things and was about to take his first step down the ladder when Sheila launched into another tirade of barking. Something in her tone made him step back onto the roof. This didn't sound like the yap she reserved for Bernie.

He was high enough to get a good view of the track leading up to the camp, and although the trees formed a natural canopy over the walkway, he could see human figures progressing through the shrub.

Visitors were rare on this part of the island. Several large 'trespassers will be prosecuted' signs kept bushwalkers out of their area.

David weighed up his options. It was too late to get back down and retrieve his licensed gun. Besides, he kept it locked up and the ammunition was in a separate part of the shed.

Ehvah was now walking up to the shed towards Pop and Sheila, probably to see what all the commotion was about.

David grabbed the box cutter he had brought to fix the cord and lay face down on the roof so he wouldn't be seen by the approaching group. He whispered down to his grandfather from his elevated position. "Hey, Pop."

The older man looked up.

"Three approaching. I'll stay up here."

"Come on over here with me, missy," Pop called over to Ehvah. "Looks like we may have some visitors."

Ehvah's big eyes widened as she spotted his head hanging over the roof gutter.

"Don't panic. I'll stay up here for now, out of sight. Stay with Pop. Don't give me away until we know who they are and what they want."

She nodded, but David could see the color drain from her face. She arrived at his grandfather's side as three people appeared in the clearing. Two men and one woman.

"What are they doing here?" Ehvah's voice was shaky.

"Who is it?" Pop asked.

"My aunt, Mara and her toyboy, Lyle. I don't know the other man."

David had never seen Ehvah's aunt. Mara looked nothing like her niece. This woman was well-built with a body that mirrored a lot of Hollywood actresses in their forties—cosmetically enhanced in all the right places. She wore a big sun hat, dark glasses, and her hair was pulled back. Her stylish outfit and shoes were inappropriate for an Australian bush walk. Wet patches under her arms and a brown stain on her white blouse suggested she had undergone some physical stress getting here.

One of the men was dressed in an upmarket city style. His slicked-back hair had fallen out of place and he ran a hand across it to smooth it out as they approached.

The other man was dressed much more casually, in a blue shirt and three-quarter length shorts. His hair was cut short and a huge diamond adorned one ear.

David felt a touch in his spirit. This was a man to watch.

"Ehvah, dear. How nice to see you." Mara's voice dripped with scorn.

Pop settled Sheila, who was frantic at his side.

"How did you find me and what do you want?" Ehvah moved her hands to her hips as they met at the corner of the shed.

"That's a lovely way to greet your only family."

The slick man David had picked as Lyle dropped a leather shoulder bag he had been carrying.

"Ehvah, you're looking well."

The way the man leered at her from top to toe set David's teeth on edge. Ehvah also must have felt vulnerable under his gaze because she crossed her arms over her body.

"Who's this?" She motioned to the other man while Sheila gave a low, rumbling growl.

"My cousin, Vinnie. Vinnie, this is Ehvah."

"We gonna do this or what?" Vinnie squinted as he glanced at his friends.

David noticed Pop stand a little taller, revealing he had also discerned the danger in Vinnie.

"I think I should be the one to talk to my niece. Besides, we haven't met this gentleman." Mara gestured to Pop.

"You don't need to know who I am, lady. Just tell us why you're here."

His straight talking had an instant effect on Mara. She took off her glasses and fixed one hand to her hip. Her eyes beamed nasty vibes at Pop while her mouth twisted into a scowl.

"If that's what you want, I'll get right to it." Mara turned to address Ehvah. "You have something of mine and I want it back."

"I don't know what you're talking about. What do I have of yours?" Ehvah shifted her weight from one foot to the other.

"Before he was killed, James transferred some money. It was the last of the inheritance from my mother. He had found out about me and Lyle, so to spite me, he was going to take off with my money as well as a heap of yours."

The shift in Mara's weight gave away the lie.

"He planted the location of this money on you. Again, I think he did this to spite me, so that I would have to come to you for help. He knew how we didn't get on."

Ehvah put one hand behind her back and gave the thumbs down sign for him to see.

"Is that right? James told me you had spent that inheritance long before you met him."

Mara gave Lyle a brief look. "Well, he lied didn't he? You're a naive little girl, Ehvah. Just give us what we want and you never have to see me again."

Ehvah's stance fixed firm as she pointed a finger at her aunt.

"You're a liar and a thief, and you're in on the whole thing. James was stealing that money for you, wasn't he? You have blood on your hands and you don't even care. All you want is money. That's all you ever wanted."

Mara took a step towards her.

"Shut up, you . . ." A slur of colorful names exited her mouth.

Vinnie counteracted Pop's advance with one of his own.

"Maybe we should move this along." He reached behind his back and pulled out a knife.

David steeled himself to jump, but Vinnie didn't advance.

"Do you know where the information is or not? If you do, you'd better tell me now."

Lyle reared back, holding his hands out to his cousin.

"Put that away, Vinnie. You . . . you know how I feel about violence. Can you at least wait until we've gone?"

Vinnie waved the knife towards him. "Shut up. Let me handle this."

Lyle cowered.

Ehvah tightened her hands into fists, while Pop moved in front of her, as a shield.

David weighed up the situation. Lyle didn't look like he would fight back and Pop could handle Mara if she got nasty, but Vinnie was still too far away from him to get in a clean jump. He would have to wait until the man moved closer towards Ehvah and Pop.

"You're too late. I've already contacted the FBI. They know all about the money and about me having the location. I've told them where it is, so you may as well leave now."

Ehvah's voice was strong. She was tapping into her fighting spirit. David held his breath, hating the fact that she was having to go through this while he waited for the perfect opportunity to jump on Vinnie.

"You stupid little . . ." Mara reeled back. "Hang on. What do you mean you told the FBI? How did they know you had the location of the money? How did you even know you had it?"

Ehvah didn't waver.

"The FBI knows everything. They've had an informer in the crime syndicate's camp for a long time. They knew about the money laundering, about James planting the location on me, and they know about you being involved. So I suggest you get out of here real quick, because they could turn up any minute."

David felt a surge of pride at the way Ehvah was handling the situation. She was standing up to them and thinking of ways to get them to leave.

Mara's mouth fell open.

"How did they find out about you having the information through the Russian mob? James sent that letter to me. We . . ." she indicated her accomplices, " . . . were the only ones who knew about your involvement."

David noticed that Lyle was silent. He fiddled with the gold belt buckle on his pants and swayed a little from side to side. Vinnie was scanning the camp from left to right.

"Hang on, where's the bodyguard?" Vinnie showed the knife blade again.

"What?" Mara's voice was so loud it echoed over the camp.

"The bodyguard she's supposed to be with. It can't be this old man. So where is he?"

Vinnie took two steps back to glance around the side of the shed. As his back twisted, Ehvah let out squeal. A black inked snake's head slithered out from under the collar of Vinnie's shirt.

"You." Ehvah pointed at him. "You killed James."

Vinnie whipped back.

"Will someone explain what is going on here?" Mara yelled.

David could see Ehvah's shoulders stiffen.

"The man who killed James had that tattoo on the back of his neck. It's him. I'm telling you, he's the murderer. He killed James. I saw him."

Mara shook her head.

"That's impossible. He didn't even know James. We involved him a week ago." She pointed a finger at Lyle. "Can you explain this?"

"I . . .. I . . ." Lyle shook from head to toe.

Vinnie stepped towards his sniveling cousin.

"You gonna tell her, or will I?"

Lyle shook his head frantically.

Vinnie curled his lip at Lyle before continuing.

"Lyle come to us for help. He knew James would give him up if the Russians asked who did the withdrawal. We saw a chance to make some easy cash. After your husband gave us the bank account number, we didn't need him no more." He stopped to spit on the ground. "Besides, I wasn't gonna take any risks with the Russians. With James dead it was an easy take. Lots of money, cut two ways, and Russian-free because they didn't know who we were."

Mara swung towards Lyle. Her torso stiffened, and her hand recoiled to strike Lyle's face.

"Cut two ways? You and this creep were going to double-cross me and take the money for yourselves? Until James gave you the wrong information. So what were you going to do when you had the location from Ehvah, Lyle? Kill me too?"

Lyle held his cheek. "No, no nothing like that. I was going to give the crime mob the location so they didn't hurt us."

Vinnie scowled at him.

"What? You didn't tell me that. You said we could get the money and cut for it."

Lyle attempted to push back a clump of hair that flopped onto his forehead. His hand was shaking so much he couldn't perform the task.

"They found me when I went back to L.A. I had to tell them about Ehvah having the location. They had worked out I was involved, and said if I didn't get the money back, they were going to kill us both."

"You are such a fool. If you hadn't stuffed up in the first place, they would never have suspected us, or found out that James had been skimming. This is all your fault. If it wasn't for your stupidity, I'd be where I wanted to be instead of stuck here in this mess."

The knife caught the sun, flashing beams of light off its surface as Vinnie tilted it towards his cousin.

"You were gonna double-cross me?"

Lyle put his head in his hands sobbed. "I'm so sorry. It all got messed up. I didn't know what to do. They're going to kill us all." The wail that followed was nothing short of pitiful.

Vinnie shook his head. "Well, what am I supposed to do now? They know I killed someone." He pointed at Ehvah and Pop.

He juggled the knife from one hand to the other, clearly considering his options. He was still too far away for David to make a successful jump on him, and the only way for Ehvah and Pop to reach safety was past the three intruders.

A slight movement at the corner of David's eye caught his attention. It was Bernie, making his way through the gutter. He was a foot away.

A plan formed in his mind.

David placed the box cutter down and reached over to take a firm hold of the snake from behind the neck.

Vinnie stepped forward, tilting the knife so that the blade was primed for attack.

David pulled at the snake. Bernie complied, remaining still as he extracted him from the gutter. He glanced towards Mara, who had moved several paces back, away from Vinnie and his weapon.

A cry of unveiled fear sounded from Lyle. His face contorted and body cowered. A wet patch made slow progress down the leg of his pants.

At the exact time Vinnie reached the spot below him, David hurled Bernie off the roof.

Vinnie's head and shoulders collapsed under the weight of the snake. He dropped the knife as he started to panic. Ironic—the man with the snake tattoo appeared to be afraid of snakes. David launched off the roof, landing on Vinnie, who had now escalated his freaking out to drastic proportions, and connected several blows that succeeded in laying him out cold. David grabbed the knife and threw it towards Pop.

David secured Vinnie's arms behind his back, then placed one knee between his shoulder blades.

"I thought you liked snakes, tough guy." He looked at Pop. "Have you got any rope handy?"

Pop gave Ehvah the knife and ran into the shed.

Lyle was crumpled on the ground, shaking. Telltale stains on his cream pants signified he was incapable of fighting back.

Bernie looked as though he had escaped unharmed. He slid over the grass towards the trees.

Mara had bolted from the scene. David caught a glimpse of her sun hat at the edge of the track. She was stuck in a wait-a-while bush. Its spindly tentacles latched onto the body, ripping her flesh and making it difficult for her to move. She thrashed about, hollering in pain and frustration. If the situation hadn't been so serious, he would have burst out laughing.

He was about to make a move to her when she escaped the tree's clutches, took a frantic look behind, and then staggered down the track and out of sight. David decided to let her go so he could concentrate on the men, and protecting Ehvah and Pop.

He used the rope to secure Vinnie, then handed a length to Pop so he could do the same with Lyle.

He moved to Ehvah, took her in his arms and held her tight until he felt her breathing stabilize. She clung to him for a moment, but as her grip softened he pulled away to kiss her forehead.

"You did great," he assured her.

She looked up to him, her huge green eyes radiating raw emotion.

"Can we call Agent Gregson back now?"

David smiled down at her. "We sure can."

CHAPTER 32

"**E**hvah, it's for you," David called out from the kitchen.

She threw the ball for Sheila one last time and ran towards the camp. David held his hand over the talking point of the cell.

"It's Gregson." He handed her the phone and walked back into the shed.

"Yes?"

"We've got her." Gregson's voice was full of jubilation. "Your aunt isn't as smart as she thinks she is. She might have been able to hide from us for the last week, but we've caught her trying to sneak out of the country. She was in Brisbane, attempting to charter a yacht to Fiji. Unfortunately she chose a skipper who was an undercover customs agent. Something about her rang warning bells, so he looked into who she was and discovered she was wanted. She's in custody. It's a small miracle."

Ehvah smiled. Prayer worked. *Thank you, Lord.*

"So what happens next?"

"We've wrapped it up. Mara and Lyle are both willing to confess everything in exchange for lesser charges. Vinnie is back in the States, up on murder. We've got his two cousins who were with him the night he shot James. They're both willing to testify against him. We've got the money—it was where you said it would be, in Mexico. Between Lyle and your aunt we have all the evidence we need against the Russian gang. It doesn't even look like we'll need you to testify. At this point, you're free to get on with your life."

Ehvah bit her lip. "What about my safety?"

"I'm sure there will be some renewed interest in you

considering the spectacular nature of the crime. We've already had considerable pressure from social commentators to release details, so no doubt they will pursue you. There will be a gag order on you until after the trial is over, so I need to warn you to not discuss any aspects of the case yet."

"I can assure you I won't be speaking to the media, and I don't have a manager or agent at the moment to pressure me into anything. Besides, I don't want to be known for this."

She had come to the conclusion that it wasn't the traumatic experiences which defined her, but how God had used them to confirm who she was and how much she meant to Him. She wanted the story to be the renewal of her faith.

"Apart from the constraints of your career, there's no reason for you to retain the heightened security. You can come down out of the hills and start living your life again."

Gregson's news had good points and bad points. Ehvah was delighted to know she was free of the burden of James's death and the mystery surrounding her involvement in the missing money. But now there was no reason for her to continue living at the camp, or have David stay with her. The second thought sent her spirits nosediving.

"Okay, thanks." She managed to conjure up the appropriate amount of joy at Gregson's news.

"I have a flight in an hour, so I have to go. You have my number if you need me." Gregson was all business again.

"Thank you for everything." Ehvah ended the call.

David walked up to her just as she pressed the disconnect button.

"Good news?"

She handed him back the cell.

"They've got Mara." She relayed all the details. "So I guess that's it. I can go back to life as I knew it."

She looked down and kicked the edge of the plywood floor of the kitchen.

"Is that what you want?" David's voice was low.

She looked up at him from under heavy eyelids. His focus was fixed on a salt shaker. He tapped the lid with one finger. Ehvah noticed the tension in his jaw.

Her mouth was dry and her heart raced at the thought of life without him. "No, not really."

"I didn't think we would stay here forever, so if you're ready to go back home, I'll understand. Don't stay here for me."

She glanced back down at the floor. His statement gave her a new wave of resolve. She took a deep breath and began to speak.

"I don't want to stay here for you. I want to be wherever God wants me to be. I want to be like my parents, and trust that He has the answers to my questions. And when bad things happen, I want to trust that He loves me more than anything. That's what I want."

He looked up at her, inspiring her heart beat heavy in her chest as his chocolate eyes captured hers.

"I want us to be together, because that's what the Lord has for both of us," she continued. "Not for any other reason. Because if there is one thing I know for sure, it's that life is too short to die wondering, and from this moment on, I don't ever want to wonder what He had for me. I want to be living it. Good times and bad."

She felt tears well. "I'm done with fear, and being stuck in a hole. I want to live, to love, and know that I'm loved for every second of it. I want us to be together and for God to use both our lives."

She couldn't stop the outpouring of her emotions any more than she could have stopped the tears.

David covered the distance between them to hold her in his arms and kiss her wet cheeks. Ehvah lifted her face to him and reveled in his love.

As he held her close and kissed her hair he said, "I couldn't think of a better plan."

She smiled into his chest and held on tight.

EPILOGUE

Ehvah entered the dressing room and ran to give her friend a hug.

"You're here."

Rhi's eyes were as wide as her smile. She looked sensational in the new outfit Ehvah had purchased for her. Designer jeans, a silk blouse, and a wicked pair of heels.

"I feel so spoilt."

"I told you I'd find somewhere flash to take you." Ehvah delighted in her young friend's enthusiasm.

"I didn't think anything would ever top my bridesmaid's dress, but this outfit is perfect for your comeback concert. Thank you, I love it." The girl's eyes glistened.

Ehvah gave her another hug. "I'm so happy you're here. I can't believe it was two weeks ago that we were on Millionaire's Row and I was getting married." She stopped to take a deep breath. "I think I'm more nervous about tonight."

Rhi fingered the floating sleeve of Ehvah's dress. "Don't be. You look like a superstar."

Ehvah detailed her reflection from head to toe.

Her stage outfit was simple, but the quality designer fabrics ensured the floating skirt and sweetheart neckline of the dress fitted her to perfection.

She glanced at the clock.

"Twenty minutes. I hope I don't cry and ruin my make-up."

"Do you want me to stick my head out and see what's going on?"

"No." Ehvah shook her head. "The stage manager will come and get me when it's time. I have no doubt it will all be under control. I hope so, anyway."

Apart from the occasional trip to meet David's family, they had spent much of their time since Mara's arrest at the Island camp, writing songs, cementing their relationship, and being stringently chaperoned by Pop. He'd been pleased when their wedding day had finally arrived, and he could 'stop being the wandering hands cop.' His reference to the way he policed the couple's physical contact had made Ehvah giggle.

Ehvah pulled out her lip gloss and applied one last cover. She stood back and scanned her reflection.

"I still can't believe how much my life has changed in six months."

Rhi's mirror image smiled behind her.

"I can't believe you and David got married and had two new singles hit the international charts in less than two weeks."

Ehvah turned to face her. "It was a lot longer than two weeks in production, but it was still fast."

There was a knock on the door and the stage manager poked his head inside.

"I have to take the young lady to her seat."

Ehvah grabbed Rhi's hand. "Your family is all here right?" Ehvah needed to know their support team was all accounted for.

Rhi rolled her eyes. "Are you kidding? They were the first ones seated. Between the wedding and your singing careers, we're all living through you both right now." Her smile indicated she was teasing.

"I can't think of any better way to spend our honeymoon." She shivered with nervous energy and gave Rhi one last good-luck hug.

As Rhi left the room, Ehvah knew she would be eternally grateful for the way Ron Murray and his family had taken her under their wings.

Rhi and her two older sisters had served as bridesmaids at her wedding. Dr. Murray's wife slipped into the role of mother-of-the-bride, while Ron did the honors as pastor. Pop relished the task of giving her away.

The intimate gathering also included David's parents, his younger brother, Nathan and his girlfriend, and extended friends, family, and army brothers. The infamous Mark had also attended, his new Russian bride-to-be in toe. Ehvah thought the girl was lovely, even though she couldn't speak a word of English.

Boof enthusiastically accepted the roll of best man after giving his begrudging agreement to their one condition—no playing the instruments.

"Are you ready?"

The stage manager re-entered the room. She gave him her best smile.

"As ready I'll ever be."

***

David checked the musical equipment one last time before pausing to feel the hum of the crowd within the grand Texan theatre.

They had expected a moderate crowd tonight, but the audience was so loud from behind the curtain that he stuck his head around the folds of material to take a look.

The place was packed. He could see Ron Murray and his family seated in the front row. Boof was there too, munching away on unidentified snack food.

Sam, their new manager, appeared over his shoulder. Sam's round face was as rotund as his body. His cheeks held a pink tinge under the heat of the stage lights, and a great smile beamed from under his bushy moustache.

"It's a big crowd tonight."

"Sure is."

"I've been looking for you so I could share some news. The album just hit number one."

A sense of gratitude rose within him.

"That's awesome. I can't believe it's only been five weeks."

Sam extracted a handkerchief from his pocket and wiped his brow.

"When both singles hit number one we all predicted the album would do well, but this is a real blessing."

David knew his beaming smile matched Sam's.

The songs he and Ehvah had written and recorded together over the last six months were a mixture of gospel and mainstream contemporary music. Their style didn't fit into a specific genre, and as a consequence they assumed the big recording labels wouldn't take a chance on them. Fortunately, the Lord already had someone in mind. The small recording company they signed with had the desire to produce music with a message. Their hope was to reach a mainstream audience and show them who Jesus was, and how His love changes lives.

Their new manager, Sam, was part of the package, and he hadn't let them down.

"I can't believe the response we've had online as well. It's been amazing." David shook his head at the wonder of it.

"God's timing is perfect." Sam nodded.

"Are we good to go?" Ehvah walked across the stage towards them. Her full skirt floated in harmony with her movement, and her high heeled boots click-clacked on the surface of the stage.

David had been backstage with her an hour ago, but each time he saw her anew, she dazzled him with her presence.

"Did I tell you how beautiful you look tonight?"

"You did, but I'll hear it again." She gave him a smile, and moved into his embrace, making him want nothing more than to smudge her pink lipstick. The wispy blond tendrils around her face fell back as she tilted her head up to him.

She rose on tiptoes and touched her lips to his, happy to chance a smudge.

The sound of Sam clearing his throat broke their moment.

"Sam just delivered some exciting news." He looked over to their manager. "Do you want to tell her?"

Sam lifted his index finger in the air. "Number one."

Ehvah's mouth fell open and her big green eyes widened. "The album?"

David nodded.

Both of her arms went in the air and she cried, "Yes."

David grabbed her waist and twirled her around. A heightened sense of elation flowed between them. They had worked hard, and the Lord was rewarding them with His plan and direction. There was no doubt music was the talent God had given him to use for His purpose. David sent up a brief prayer of thanks for Ehvah and the miraculous way she had been brought into his life to remind him of what he loved.

He placed her feet back on the floor and lifted the curtain a little to the side.

"Have a look. Full house."

Ehvah peeked through the slit.

She looked back, emerald eyes sparkling.

***

Ehvah had to mentally pinch herself following Sam's news of their number one status. She released a happy sigh as she took her place on a high stool next to David's at the front of the stage. The set was primed for their opening song. Never in her wildest dreams could she have anticipated the life she was leading.

Ehvah thought back to the first moment she had met her husband. She was running from danger, her life in limbo, and her spirit in turmoil. Yet her time in Australia had been one of the happiest times of her life. She had turned to God, given the fear to Him, and learned to trust in the plan He had for her life.

She and David had penned seven of the twelve songs on their album at the camp. The other songs had been written by her parents, part of the unrecorded portfolio released to her when she had come into her trust fund that year. They had written the songs so long ago, yet each one was in tune with where her life was right now. It was their gift to her, and recording them to share with the world was her gift to them. God's love running full circle, His grace and purpose at work.

The inclusion of her parent's songs on the album, as well as the heightened interest in her life, had drawn a readymade audience.

She and David made a powerful writing team, and their

relationship grew stronger every day. Even with the stresses and changing nature of the music business, and now a touring lifestyle, their faith had brought them closer together.

Ehvah looked down at the rings on her finger. David, and all his people were her family now. She was their daughter.

They had a list of touring dates before they would see Pop again. She missed the peace and raw tranquility of her adopted homeland. Australia had started off as place to escape to, yet now it was her second home.

The stage manager signaled to them from the side of the stage.

Ehvah looked over at her husband. "I love you."

He leaned over and touched his lips to hers in a tender kiss. "I love you too, baby."

She held out her hand and took his as they bent their heads and prayed that the music they were about to perform would touch the hearts of the audience and show each and every listener who Jesus was.

David picked up his guitar while she positioned her microphone.

As the curtain opened, the starting notes of the song her parents wrote for her all those years ago rang out from David's guitar. Their first number one hit. *Ehvah After.*

About the Author

Rose, who holds a Bachelor of Arts Degree, was born in North Queensland, Australia. Her childhood experiences growing up in a small beach community would later provide inspiration for her first novel, Back to Resolution.

Her novels are inspired by the love of her coastal home and desire to produce exciting and contemporary stories of faith for women.

Beyond Resolution and A New Resolution are the second and third books in the Resolution series.

Rose's debut novel Back to Resolution won the Bookseller's Choice award at the 2012 CALEB Awards, while A New Resolution won the 2013 CALEB Prize for Fiction.

She has also released The Greenfield Legacy, a collaborative novel, written in conjunction with three other outstanding Australian authors.

Rose resides in Mackay, North Queensland with her husband, young son, and mischievous pup, Noodle.

http://rosedee.com/
https://www.facebook.com/pages/Rose-Dee-Author/172886062810998

Other Titles:

Back to Resolution
Beyond Resolution
A New Resolution
The Greenfield Legacy

Please note:
The referred book dealing with Post-Traumatic Stress

Disorder in this story is fictional.

If you would like more information regarding the treatment of Post-Traumatic Stress Disorder, and incorporating Christian Counselling please find some helpful links below.

Australia: Christian Counsellors Association Australia. http://www.ccaa.net.au/

North America: American Association of Christian Counsellors. http://www.aacc.net/

United Kingdom: Association of Christian Counsellors. http://www.acc-uk.org/